BOOKS BY KRISTI D. HOLL

JUST LIKE A REAL FAMILY
MYSTERY BY MAIL
FOOTPRINTS UP MY BACK
THE ROSE BEYOND THE WALL
FIRST THINGS FIRST
CAST A SINGLE SHADOW
PERFECT OR NOT, HERE I COME
THE HAUNTING OF CABIN 13
PATCHWORK SUMMER

PATCHWORK SUMMER

PATCHWORK SUMMER

KRISTI D. HOLL

ATHENEUM

1987

NEW YORK

Atheneum
Macmillan Publishing Company
866 Third Avenue, New York, NY 10022
Collier Macmillan Canada, Inc.

Type set by Arcata Graphics/Kingsport, Kingsport, Tennessee
Printed and bound by Fairfield Graphics, Fairfield, Pennsylvania
Designed by Christine Kettner
First Edition
10 9 8 7 6 5 4 3 2 1

Library of Congress Cataloging-in-Publication Data

Holl, Kristi D.
Patchwork summer.

Summary: When her mother suddenly returns home a
year after having walked out on her family, thirteen-year-
old Randi tries hard to conquer her own anger and
feelings of being permanently scarred by the experience.
[1. Mothers and daughters—Fiction] I. Title.
PZ7.H7079Pat 1987   [Fic]   86-32107
ISBN 0-689-31347-0

FOR LAURIE

CONTENTS

PATCHWORK
SUMMER

1
■

RUNAWAY MOM

Randi McBride wrinkled her nose, trying to breathe without actually inhaling. The rubbing-alcohol smell of the doctor's office always made her stomach turn.

She clutched the wrinkled pages of a magazine that had been left on her chair. "What am I doing here, anyway?" she mumbled. It was supposed to be a *mother's* job to coax little kids in for their kindergarten checkups.

Randi sighed. She might be too young for the role, but playing mother was nothing new anymore. In fact, these days it was hard for her to remember she was only thirteen years old.

"Hey, Randi, look at this," her sister called.

Glancing up, Randi forced herself to smile. Meggie held out a plastic Mr. Potato Head, with the black pipe sticking out of one ear and the bright red lips perched on top of his potato skull.

Randi raised her voice above the racket in the Tiny Tots Corner. "That's funny, Meggie. Do another one."

3

Grinning, Meggie yanked out the pieces, then proceeded to stick eyeballs in the ear slots and the top hat in the mouth slot. Beside her, a toddler with a runny nose chewed on Meggie's sleeve.

Out of the corner of her eye, Randi watched Meggie play. Even if her sister was a little old for those baby toys, Randi was grateful for anything that took her mind off the shot that was coming. Meggie had had such a tough year already, without having to get boosters. She had always been terrified of those long, shiny needles.

Slouching down in her fake leather chair, Randi returned to flipping through the magazine. One article caught her eye: "Runaway Teens: How to Spot the Signs." She skimmed the list, then tossed the magazine down.

No help here, she thought.

Maybe she should write her own version of the article. "Runaway Mothers: How to Spot the Signs." Bitterly, Randi decided she wasn't qualified to write it. Even after a full year of racking her brain, she couldn't remember any clues that had pointed to her mom's plans to leave.

Randi glanced at the table beside her, then automatically straightened all the battered copies of *Parents, American Baby,* and *Reader's Digest.* She made two neat stacks, squared the corners, then centered a potted fern exactly in the middle.

"Megan McBride. Megan McBride." The nurse's nasal voice twanged over the intercom. Meggie jerked back in alarm, dropping Mr. Potato Head with a clatter.

"Come on." Randi steeled herself, then took Meggie's quivering hand and led her to the nurse. "This won't take long. When you're done, I'll buy you a double chocolate cone on the way home."

"Really?"

"Sure, if you try not to cry when you get your shot."

Meggie's hair fell over one eye as she chewed her thumbnail. "I won't cry."

Striding along in whispery-soled white shoes, the nurse led them to Examining Room 3. "Dr. Benoit will be with you in a moment," she said with a professional smile as starched as her uniform. "Have your sister remove her shirt and shorts, so we can weigh and measure her." Backing out, she pulled the door closed.

Randi pointed a finger at Meggie and grinned. "You heard her. Peel 'em off."

Shivering in the cold blast from the overhead air-conditioning vent, Meggie undressed, then crawled up onto the metal examining table. It was covered with white paper that crackled. "When will I get the shot?" she asked in a small voice.

"Just before we leave, if I remember right." Randi folded Meggie's top, noticing the cookie crumbs that spilled from the pockets. "They don't want you bawling through the whole checkup, if you're the kind that cries." She smoothed Meggie's stray curls back off her face, then refastened her unicorn barrette. "But you're brave, and it'll be quick."

A light tap sounded on the door. "Everybody decent?" Dr. Benoit called out.

Randi opened the door. "Come on in." She held her breath and glanced at her little sister, who was twisting a strand of hair around her first finger.

Dr. Benoit rolled his swivel stool over to the examining table. "All set for kindergarten, Meggie?" he asked. "Hard to believe it's the first of June already. Before we know it, you'll trot off to school right beside Randi."

Meggie didn't answer, but he kept up his friendly chatter while he examined her spine, shoulders, eyes, and teeth. "Time to lie down now."

Randi smiled encouragingly at Meggie and nodded.

Chewing her lip, Meggie finally scrunched down on her back. "Is it time for the shot, Dr. Ben?" She rubbed her plump arms, covered with goosebumps.

"In a minute. Let's listen to your heart and lungs first." He rubbed the stethoscope on his plaid shirt to warm it up, then placed it on her chest. "Take some big, deep breaths."

In the hushed examining room, Randi listened to Meggie's forced breathing. Down the hall, a baby could be heard screaming.

"Ticking right along, clear as a bell." The doctor helped Meggie to a sitting position, placed the stethoscope on her back, then punched a button on the intercom. "Janice? Meggie's ready to be weighed."

Meggie slid down from the table when the nurse appeared and stared at the floor, her hands behind her back. Randi gave her a gentle push, and Meggie left with the nurse. From across the hall came a dull *klu-thunk, klu-thunk* as the nurse adjusted the weights on the scale.

Dr. Benoit rolled his stool near Randi's chair. "Well, how are things going at home?" he asked quietly.

Head down, Randi pulled at a loose thread on Meggie's shorts. "Oh, about the same. Mom's still gone, but we're used to it now."

"How's Meggie doing? Starting school this fall will be another huge adjustment for her." He combed his fingers through his scraggly reddish gray beard. "I'd hoped your dad would bring her today. There's something I need to discuss with him."

"He's at work, but you can tell me." Randi clasped her suddenly icy hands. "Meggie's with me 'most all the time."

Dr. Benoit got up to close the door. "All right." He leaned against the corner of his desk. "There are some things you need to watch for. In a few months, when summer's almost over, be alert for certain behavior."

"Like what?"

"If Meggie has trouble sleeping, or won't eat, or . . . cries a lot, give me a call." He paused, then patted Randi's shoulder. "Your mother's leaving was a big shock for her to get used to. If it used up her reserves, starting school might be doubly hard for her."

"I expected that. During Kindergarten Roundup, she wouldn't let me go home the first day when the other mothers left. I stayed the whole day, sitting in the corner."

Dr. Benoit smiled, his dark eyes crinkling at the corners. "You're going to be a terrific mother someday. Meggie's lucky to have you."

Suddenly the door flew open, and Meggie was back, waving a grape sucker.

"Look," Meggie whispered, sticking her forearm under Randi's nose. "There's holes poked in my arm."

Randi studied the four pinpricks on her skin. "What's this from?"

The nurse handed her a stamped postcard. "I gave Megan a TB skin test. It's routine. Some children have a reaction to it, however."

Randi glanced up sharply. "What kind of reaction?"

"With some children a small bump appears. It isn't painful. She also might run a slight temperature." She pointed to the four pictures on the card. "After seventy-two hours, check which illustration looks most like Megan's arm. Then circle that picture and mail the postcard to us."

Randi nodded. "That sounds simple enough."

Dr. Benoit moistened a cotton ball with alcohol. "Hop back up on the table now, Meggie. We'll get this DPT booster done, and then you'll be finished."

Meggie backed up against the wall, mesmerized by the needle in the nurse's hand. Without taking her eyes from it, she inched around behind Randi.

The nurse frowned slightly, but Randi just shrugged at

her. She had been afraid this would happen. She knelt in front of Meggie. "Hey, we talked all about this at home. The shot'll keep you from getting sick later."

Meggie's lower lip trembled.

"Come on. I'll hold your hand." Randi hoisted Meggie onto the table. Standing out of the nurse's way, she gripped her sister's hand. "Just look at me."

Meggie's panic-stricken eyes focused on Randi, and the nurse moved in. Meggie winced sharply, and tears welled up in her eyes, but she blinked them back. In a flash the doctor had a small Band-Aid over the spot and was lifting her down from the table.

Randi handed Meggie her clothes and gave her a quick hug. "See? I knew you'd be brave. Now, let's go get that ice cream!"

That evening, when her dad's car pulled into the driveway, Randi hurried to dish up supper. The minute her dad walked in the door, he expected to eat.

"Meggie, Dad's home!" she yelled down to the basement, where her sister was feeding her cat, T.C. "Come to the table."

She flipped the hamburgers one last time, drained the grease, and turned off the stove. Grabbing hot mitts, she took the baked potatoes and a dish of mixed vegetables from the microwave. Megan was seated at the table and Randi was pouring their milk by the time Mike McBride, their father, charged through the kitchen door.

"How're my girls today?" their dad boomed. "Miss me?" He hugged Randi and tickled Megan. "How's my best girl? What'd you do today?"

"Randi got me some ice cream after—"

"Guess what happened to me today?" He yanked off his paisley tie, rocking back and forth on the balls of his feet. "A young couple came in—they're building a new house—and they bought *all* their new appliances from me! Stove, refrigerator, trash compactor, dishwasher, washer-dryer combo. They just couldn't say no to me!" He plopped down at the table, making the ice in the glasses rattle.

"That's really great!" Randi said.

"That's a chunk of commission, let me tell you." Their father split open a baked potato and filled the steamy opening with butter. " 'Course, you know your dad's a darned good salesman, don't you?"

Randi nodded and grinned. They ought to know. He told them often enough. She dished up a spoonful of vegetables for Meggie. "Eat just a few bites," Randi whispered. "You won't learn to like anything new if you don't taste it."

"Yuck. If I eat all this, I won't have room for dessert." Meggie picked out the lima beans and flattened each one with her spoon. Her face brightening, she tried again. "Daddy, guess what? Today I didn't even cry when—"

"Good! Don't need any crybabies around here, do we?" Mr. McBride poured a pool of ketchup on his plate. "What was I saying? Oh, yes, that couple said they'd tell all their friends about me. Who knows? I'll probably have to open my own appliance store soon! Maybe a whole chain of stores!"

Randi nodded, only half-listening. Her dad was a lovable guy, but he could drag on for hours telling about his workday. Had he always talked so much, Randi wondered, even before her mom left them? She didn't think so, but she couldn't remember. It hadn't been her job to listen to him then.

"Meggie was brave at the doctor's today," Randi blurted out when her dad stopped long enough to eat a bite of hamburger. "She's all set for registration now."

"You're getting to be such a big girl," Mr. McBride said. "Your mother'll be so proud of you."

The corners of Randi's mouth twisted down. "Mom won't even remember Meggie starts school in the fall. She's too wrapped up playing 'Famous Author' to think about *us* anymore."

"Not true. Not true." Their dad waved his fork through the air like a magic wand. "In fact, I have an announcement. I was going to save the news for later, but I might as well tell you now."

"Tell us what?" Meggie demanded eagerly.

Rocking back in his chair, he puffed out his chest importantly. "Your mother was in the store today, and she's finally come to her senses," he said, beating a drum roll on the table with his knife and fork. "She's moving back home on Friday."

"*What?*" Randi's hand jerked, knocking over her glass of milk. The white rivulet flowed across the table, heading for her dad's lap. Jumping back, he let it dribble on the floor. Randi grabbed a dishtowel to mop it up.

"Is Mommy really coming home? Or is this just another visit?" Meggie demanded. She twisted a lock of hair around her finger, leaving flecks of potato in the curls.

"Your mother knows she made a big mistake, and she's coming back for good." Mr. McBride shoveled in a spoonful of vegetables, then pointed his spoon at Randi. "Plan a special meal for Friday night. When we welcome her home, we want to do it up right."

A chunk of hamburger lodged in Randi's throat and refused to budge. Eyes watering, she ran to the sink for a glass of water. While Meggie and her dad made plans, Randi stumbled back and forth across the kitchen clearing the table. Seething, she banged the frying pan into the sink and ran water in it full force.

She couldn't believe it. *She just couldn't believe it.*

After a whole year's absence, her mom planned to walk

10

right back into their lives. Just like that, coming home as suddenly as she'd left, like a bolt out of the blue. How could she? Did she think they'd forgotten what she'd done?

Not me, Randi thought bitterly.

She'd never forget that day a year ago when she'd found the note. With just a few short words, her mom had torn the family apart—as if she'd thrown a hand grenade into the house, then escaped before the explosion. The past year had been the worst time Randi could remember, as she'd struggled to glue the fragments of her life back together. But the old pieces just didn't fit anymore. Although Randi tried desperately to hide it, she felt scarred for life.

As she splashed the lemony dish soap into frothy bubbles, Randi studied Meggie's excited face and her father's pleased smile. They seemed delighted that Marilyn McBride had graciously decided to return home. But Randi wasn't. As far as she was concerned, it was too late. She felt just like Humpty Dumpty. All the king's horses and all the king's men couldn't put Randi together again.

With jerky movements, she wiped off the stove and flowered plastic tablecloth. Her dad had left the kitchen; the TV already blared in the living room. Meggie sat hunched over, pushing her mixed vegetables around her plate.

"Better finish up," Randi said. "Can't you eat more of your meat? You need the protein, you know. Dr. Ben said you're a growing girl."

"I'm too excited to eat," Meggie said. "Mommy's coming home! Thinking about it's making my stomach all jumpy."

Randi could understand that. Her own stomach was turning somersaults. "Go on, then. Get into your PJ's." She picked up Meggie's nearly full plate. "But just this once. After tonight, you have to clean your plate like always."

"Okay." Meggie skipped across the kitchen, then darted

back to grab Randi around the waist. "Mommy's really coming home. Isn't it wonderful?" She jumped up and down, landing on Randi's toes.

"Uh . . . sure." Randi tucked a stray curl behind Meggie's ear, then gave her a gentle push. "Now get ready for bed."

With a deep sigh, Randi drained the dirty dishwater and wiped out the sink. She envied Meggie's innocent ability to still believe in "happily ever after." As for herself, the child in her had died sometime during the past year. She was now thirteen, going on forty.

Randi wadded the dishcloth into a tight ball. She could thank only one person for this premature old age: her runaway mother.

2
■

HOMECOMING

Randi would never forget finding that horrible note. Exactly a year ago, she'd raced home, sweaty hair plastered to her face. She was ready to celebrate getting out of crabby Mrs. Binford's seventh-grade class. It had been the first week of June. Summer vacation at last!

She had burst through the kitchen door and called, "Mom, I'm home!"

Her only answer was the hollow echo in the cool house. Racing through the kitchen, she had tossed her tattered report card on the table. There Randi spotted two notes, each sealed in its own light blue envelope. One was addressed to her dad, the other to her.

Even to this day, fragments of the note still burned in her mind: I know you'll understand . . . take care of Megan . . . Dad will explain. . . . All empty, meaningless words, in her mom's neat handwriting. Randi *hadn't* understood her mom's running away, and her dad certainly couldn't explain it.

13

Following the instructions in the note like a programmed robot, Randi had collected Meggie from the neighbors who had been watching her. Starting that day, Randi would be home for the summer to take care of her four-year-old sister.

Each day for two weeks, Randi expected to see her mom walk through the front door. But as the hot summer weeks came and went, her hopes died, little by little. By fall, Randi had given up on her mom's ever coming back. She had registered herself for eighth grade, then found Mrs. Wangston to baby-sit Meggie during the day. All during the school year, Randi walked ten blocks out of her way after school to pick up her sister.

A sudden blast from the TV made Randi jump. Shaking her head, she muttered, "I'd better remember to call Mrs. Wangston." If their mom came home to stay, they wouldn't need a baby-sitter, even for the mornings after Meggie started kindergarten.

Looking down, Randi realized she had been wiping out the dry sink for several minutes. She folded the dishcloth neatly, then pulled her Betty Crocker *Cookbook for Kids* from the shelf to plan Friday night's menu. Randi clenched her jaw until her teeth ached. The meal was going to be terrific, just like her dad wanted, but *not* to make the "welcome home" special.

Randi had reasons of her own. "I'll show Mom we've gotten along just fine without her," she mumbled.

The first months after her mom deserted them, Randi had been in shock, trying to cope with everything. Her dad wandered around in his own personal fog, barely speaking, working longer and longer hours at the store. So Randi had taught herself to cook simple meals and keep house while taking care of Meggie. The work wasn't hard—there was just so much to do! Finally, by drawing charts and making a written laundry schedule, she managed to guarantee clean socks and underwear at least five days out of seven.

She flipped open the cookbook her dad had bought her for Christmas. "Now, let's see . . . Chili Mexicali? Hamburger Stroganoff?" Frowning, she turned the pages. "I know! I'll make this."

It would be perfect for Friday night. She had cooked several complicated recipes, and this was one of Meggie's favorites. It was a fancy meatloaf frosted with mashed potatoes, then topped with melted cheese. Her mom ought to be impressed with *that*.

Locking the back door, Randi headed upstairs. As she passed through the house, she noted with satisfaction that Meggie's toys and her dad's newspapers were picked up, the piano keys dusted, and the ferns thick and green. It wasn't easy to get it all done. To find a routine that worked, it had taken Randi months of trial and error.

It was worth it, though. Keeping the house neat gave Randi a feeling of order, as if she had her life under control, at least in one area.

Housework was still a pain, but Randi did enjoy being in charge. Now that she was used to running things, she intended to keep the house under her own control. Her mom wasn't going to come home and take over again. Randi shook her head firmly. No way. Who knew how long her mother would stick around, anyway? You couldn't exactly trust her.

"Randi! Help me!"

Randi took the stairs two at a time. In the bedroom they shared, she found Meggie stuck half-in and half-out of her granny pajamas. Her arms waved frantically over her head. "Get me out of here!" she cried, her voice muffled.

"Wait a minute. Don't strangle yourself." With a quick movement, Randi untangled the buttons from the short hairs at the back of her neck and slid the pajamas over Meggie's head. "There you go."

"Thanks." She flopped down on the floor to pull on her pink bunny slippers. "Randi, why did Mommy leave us?"

"We've talked about this a million times. I've told you everything I know."

"Tell me again?"

Randi sighed as she studied her little sister. Meggie clutched a brown stuffed dog, a yellow scarf now tied around its head. The scarf was their mother's, and Meggie had found it right after she left. Ever since, the scarf went everywhere with Meggie. Sometimes it was disguised as a doll blanket, or a dust cloth, or a sling for a "broken arm."

Collapsing on her bed, Randi pulled Meggie onto her lap. "Well, you know Mom sold her first book last winter, right? She didn't sell anything when she still lived at home, but writing mattered a lot to her."

"But why did she go away? She could write books here."

Randi shrugged, running fingers through her short black hair. She'd gone over this so many times before. "She said she could write better if she didn't have to spend all her time cooking and cleaning and doing our laundry. So she moved in with her writer friend. We treated her like a maid, she said."

"Oh." Meggie squirmed around, her nose just inches from Randi's face. "Does Mommy still love us?"

"Of course she does. Just like always," Randi said, figuring God would forgive her for a small lie. "She couldn't live here anymore, that's all."

"But she's coming back now. Daddy said so."

"Maybe she's ready to work at home now. She'll probably tell us Friday." She stared over Meggie's head and out the window. It was nearly dusk.

"I can't wait." Meggie snuggled down in Randi's lap. "I just can't wait."

Randi held her close. She wished things could turn out just like Meggie wanted, but she knew they'd never again be one big, happy family. The only place *that* happened was in reruns on TV.

As soon as her dad left for work the next morning, Randi wandered from room to room, pad and pencil in hand. She noted the jobs that needed to be done before Friday. The house would look spectacular, or she'd die trying. She'd show her mom they'd gotten along just fine without her. No matter what, Randi never intended to let her mom know what a rough year it had been.

Or how much her leaving had hurt.

An hour later her list was overwhelmingly long. She hadn't noticed before, but smudgy fingerprints clouded the windows and the dingy curtains needed washing. The kitchen and bathroom floors needed to be mopped; the dusty philodendron leaves could use waxing. Randi chewed the eraser on her pencil. All the extra work would have to be added to the usual vacuuming and laundry, but some-how she'd manage.

For three days Randi worked like a slave. By Friday night she was ready to drop from exhaustion, but the house sparkled. The white eyelet curtains were crisp, and the windows were so clean they almost disappeared. In a way, she was grateful for the extra scrubbing, polishing, and ironing. It had kept her mind from going too often to her mother—and what her coming home might mean. Now, if she could just finish the frosted meatloaf before her mother arrived. . . .

"Daddy's home!" Meggie yelled from the living room, where she kept watch at the window. "When's Mommy coming?" she wailed for the hundredth time.

17

"Pretty soon." Sweat broke out on Randi's upper lip as she stirred the instant potatoes. Scooping them out, she carefully frosted the round meatloaf with the potatoes. Soon the platter held one large white mound.

Whistling, her dad bounded through the door. "Mmm, that smells good, honey." He patted her shoulder. "Look what I picked up on the way home. You know me—the last of the big-time spenders!" He pushed a bouquet of red roses under her nose.

"They're beautiful." Randi jerked her head to the left. "The vases are up in that cupboard."

After carefully arranging five triangles of cheese on top of the potatoes, she set the platter in the microwave. She had just finished the cinnamon dressing for the fruit salad when a car turned the corner at the end of the block.

Randi's hand stopped in midair. She would know the sound of those screechy brakes anywhere. A second later Meggie screamed, "Mommy's home! Mommy's home!" and tore through the kitchen and out the back door.

With a deep breath, Randi turned to her dad. He smiled uncertainly, smoothed down his hair and straightened his new tie, then opened the door. A minute later Marilyn McBride stood on the threshold, holding Meggie in her arms.

"Hi, everybody!" She swept into the room. "Everything smells so good! And flowers!" She bent over the bouquet in the center of the table.

"We're, uh, glad you're back," Randi's dad said, suddenly tongue-tied. He stepped forward to kiss her lightly on the cheek. "We all are," he added.

Not all of us, Randi thought. She despised her mother. Who did she think she was, anyway? Walking out a year ago, destroying their lives, then waltzing back in like she'd just returned from the corner grocery store.

Her mother turned toward Randi, her long brown hair

swinging across one eye. "Hello, Miranda. How are you?"

Randi stared at her mother's left ear. "Hi."

"Everything looks so nice. I can see you're a great help to your father."

"It's not so hard." Her voice was cutting, and Randi tried to lighten her tone. She wanted to sound as if the past year had been a snap. "As soon as everyone sits down, we can eat."

Randi straightened the silverware one last time, then set the food on the table. Her dad pulled out a chair for her mother. "Goodness, you'll all spoil me," she said with a giggle.

"We just love you, Mommy." Meggie reached for her mother's hand.

"Oh, sweetie." Marilyn gazed around the kitchen and sighed. "It's good to be home."

As she put the pitcher of iced tea back in the refrigerator, Randi studied her family. She was nauseated by the way they were treating her mother, as if she were an honored guest. Had they forgotten the awful thing she'd done?

Well, Randi remembered. *Clearly.*

She gritted her teeth till her jaw ached. Randi hadn't forgotten all the pain her mother had caused, and she'd never forgive her, either. No, not in a million years.

3
∎
ALEX

Randi made train tracks through her mashed potatoes and tried to ignore the conversation. Nothing her mom had to say was of any interest to Randi whatsoever.

"I'm sure you wonder why I decided to come home, after I'd been gone so long," her mother said.

They froze. No one moved or answered. Randi raised her left eyebrow, hoping she looked skeptical.

The silence stretched on until Meggie ventured an answer. "You missed us too much?"

Marilyn McBride blinked, then smiled and took more salad. "That, too, of course, but there were other reasons." She licked her spoon. "This dressing is very good, Miranda. Where did you get the recipe?"

"From a cookbook. It's simple enough to make." Randi usually loved it, but tonight her food sat like a rock in her stomach. "And please call me Randi now—everybody does."

"Oh, I couldn't! Miranda is such a lovely name. Nicknames are so common." Her mom smiled brightly at each of them. "I carefully chose your names so we'd all have the same initials. Michael McBride. Marilyn McBride. Miranda McBride. Megan McBride."

"I don't care. I hate the name Miranda. I always have," Randi muttered.

Her dad rubbed his hands together nervously, his large biceps flexed. "Um, you said there were reasons that made you decide to come home?"

Their mother nodded, dabbing at her mouth with a napkin. "When I lived here, no one gave a thought to how I felt; therefore, I had to. So I left. The good news is that I finally found myself."

Mr. McBride tapped his knife on the edge of his plate. "Um, found yourself?"

"You know what I mean. Now that I have a book coming out this summer, I've proved that I'm serious about my writing."

Randi glanced up briefly. "Baloney."

"Miranda!" Her father's voice was sharp.

About to say more, Randi caught the terrified expression on Meggie's face. She bit her tongue. "I'm sorry," she muttered.

But she wasn't sorry. She thought her mother was handing them a bunch of crap. There was more to her reason for coming home than having "found herself." Randi would bet on it.

Her dad smiled weakly at his wife. "How's Stella these days?" he asked.

Their mom had met Stella in an adult writing class. Living in nearby Union, Stella had offered to share an apartment if Marilyn wanted to move in with her. It hadn't taken two weeks for their mother to agree.

"Oh, Stella's a little out of sorts. She quit her secretarial job to work at the apartment, doing freelance writing—

brochures, resumes, that sort of thing." Lifting her shoulder-length hair, she rubbed the back of her neck. "Actually, once I sold my book, things were never quite the same. I think she's jealous."

Meggie slid down from her chair and inched around the table. Shyly, she patted her mother's arm. "I'm so glad you're home."

"Have you missed me?" her mother asked. "Really?"

"Oh, yes!" Meggie climbed up into her lap and wrapped her arms around her neck. "I like to hug you even better than my cat."

Randi was startled by an acute stab of jealousy. Meggie had been her constant shadow for a whole year. Now, as soon as their mom walked through the door, it was as if all Randi's time and attention hadn't mattered at all.

Mr. McBride pushed back from the table. "Why don't we have our dessert in the living room? That is, if you'd like to? Miranda can bring in the cake, can't you, honey?" Bouncing lightly on the balls of his feet, he held his wife's chair. "Come rest awhile. I'll tell you what I've been doing at work; then we can bring in your bags."

Their mother carried Meggie out of the kitchen. "Great supper," she called over her shoulder. When they reached the living room, Randi heard her say, "Wow! It's spotless. I see you've finally learned to function without being waited on hand and foot."

Randi fumed inwardly. She never remembered her mom being a slave, but the house *did* look spotless. Even the warm kitchen still looked tidy, in spite of the unwashed dishes. Randi inspected the room quickly. She liked to keep things neat and in order, under control. Noticing the messy spice rack, she quickly turned all the small glass jars so the labels faced forward.

Prying off the plastic cake cover, Randi sliced the two-layer spice cake, careful to give her mother an extra big slice. That should convince her what a great cook she had become. The last thing they needed was for her mom to step in and take over again.

Randi nodded grimly. They had been getting along just fine.

After hours of nightmares, Randi woke the next morning with a knot in her stomach the size of a baseball. When she heard her dad's car pull out of the driveway, the knot tightened. Pressing hard against her stomach, she stared at the ceiling. Every morning for a year Randi had wakened with the same thought: *Mom ran away.* Now, this morning, a second thought followed immediately: *Mom's back.*

Why did both thoughts make her equally mad?

Dragging herself to a sitting position, Randi reached for Muddy, a stuffed monkey she had had for years. Made from men's dark knit socks, it was stuffed with old nylons. Pieces of panty hose poked out through tiny holes in the ragged tail. Cuddling the monkey close, Randi was glad she had kept him. It helped to have something to reach for during long, sleepless nights.

Rubbing the back of her neck, Randi stared at Meggie, asleep across the room. Her chubby fingers clutched the old yellow scarf, gripped tightly even in sleep.

Randi tiptoed to the door and down the hall to the kitchen. The house was quiet; evidently her mom was still sleeping.

Yawning, she ran fingers through her chopped-off black hair while looking through the cupboards. She finally decided to make raisin pancakes for Meggie. To a small packet of instant pancake mix, Randi added milk and stirred.

After tossing in a handful of raisins and heating the griddle, she poured four small pancakes. Turning, she was startled to find her mother watching from the doorway.

"That looks good. Is there any orange juice?"

"In the refrigerator. I make it the night before so it's cold in the morning."

"Very efficient." Her mother tightened the belt on her terry bathrobe, poured herself a glass, and sat down at the table. "Want any help there?"

"No. I've made these at least a hundred times. They're Meggie's favorite." Feeling smug, she expertly flipped the pancakes.

"Well, then, I'll go wake Megan up."

"Forget it. She'll wake up when she smells the pancakes." Randi spoke more curtly than she had intended, but she wasn't sorry.

"I guess you're right." They could hear Megan's bare feet padding down the hall. "Of course, Megan's grown a bit plump lately. Boiled eggs or plain toast would be better for her than pancakes."

Randi whipped around at the stove, her eyes narrowed to slits. "Just be glad she's eating," she hissed. Her voice was barely more than a whisper, but filled with venom. "After you walked out, it was a month before I could get her to eat more than a bite or two of anything."

Hands shaking, Randi scooped up the pancakes with a spatula, then poured four more. Oh, she knew her mom was right. Meggie *was* getting pretty round, but it wasn't just from eating too much at mealtimes. Randi knew Meggie was sneaking food. She found cookie crumbs under Meggie's pillow when she made the beds. She discovered candy wrappers in her pockets when sorting laundry. She had even spotted her tasting the cat food once.

Over the past six months, whenever she had that hollow, sad look in her eyes, Meggie always asked for food. No matter how doubtful she felt, Randi could never say no. As much as Meggie had been hurt, fixing treats for her was the least Randi could do.

A minute later Meggie bounced into the room to find

her pancakes already buttered. "Oh, good! I thought I smelled pancakes," Meggie said, sliding onto her chair. She pulled down the yellow scarf that had covered her nose and mouth like a bandit's. "Randi always makes me what I want. She cooks good."

"I can see that. I've almost forgotten how, myself. Stella and I ate a lot of hamburgers and frozen TV dinners." She ruffled Megan's hair. "However, tonight I'll fix you something really special. You've always loved spaghetti, and I'd enjoy cooking again."

Randi plunked down the plate of extra pancakes on the table. "Tacos are Meggie's favorite meal now," she said flatly. "I already planned those for supper." She glared at her mother, waiting to be contradicted.

Instead, Marilyn said, "Well, that sounds good, too. Since you have things so well in hand, I'll spend the day arranging my office." She carefully peeled some dry skin from her thumb.

"Office?" Randi said, taken by surprise. "You're renting an office?"

"No, I'll clear the junk out of the sewing room, then put my typewriter and supplies in there." She buttered another pancake and poured on the syrup. "Now that I'm a real writer, I need an office where I can work and not be disturbed."

Meggie jerked up in alarm, a piece of pancake falling out of her mouth. "We won't bother you, Mommy. Honest we won't." Her expression was one of pure panic as she searched Randi's face. "We won't bother her anymore, will we?"

Randi studied her little sister's face. How quickly the old terror came flooding back!

"No, we won't bother her." She patted Meggie's arm. "Mom won't have to run away to *find herself* again."

Her mother glanced up sharply, but Randi continued

eating. The pancake had stuck in her throat, but she'd never let her mother know how hard it was to eat at the same table with her. She wouldn't give her the satisfaction.

When Meggie skipped off to give T.C. a pancake, and her mom to clean up the sewing room, Randi stacked the dirty dishes in the sink. Running hot water, she was surprised at both the relief and the anger that boiled up inside her, in almost equal amounts.

She was relieved by her mother's "hands-off" attitude. Randi had expected to have to fight her mother's takeover. However, her mom seemed glad to let Randi run the house and make the decisions, just as she had in her year-long absence. But for some reason, that infuriated Randi, too. Why should she be stuck with all the cooking and cleaning, just because her mother had "found herself"?

The *clink-thunk* of metal on metal snapped her out of her thoughts. The mailman was early, Randi noted, wiping her hands on a faded dishtowel. Sliding down the hall in her stockinged feet, she saw her mom had already beaten her to the front door.

With her back held stiffly, Marilyn sorted through the stack of mail. "Here's something for you, Miranda." She peered at the envelope. "The return says Alex somebody, in Newport. That's not little Alexander Woodleaf from next door, is it?"

Randi snatched the letter. "Yes."

"What's he doing in Newport?"

Randi gave her mom a level look, wishing she could come right out and say it was none of her business. No matter how much she might wish otherwise, the days of being honest with her mother were long over. "He's visiting his dad and stepmother for the summer." She paused, then couldn't help adding, "You remember his dad. He ran away from home, too, a few years ago." She turned sharply and took the letter to her room.

Curled up on the bed, Randi ripped open the smudged letter. Alex had promised to write as soon as he got to Newport, but she was surprised he had remembered. They had been best friends this past year, and Randi didn't think she would have survived without him.

See, McBride? Told you I'd write as soon as I got here. Bet you didn't believe me.

Dad and Lois and the brats met me at the airport yesterday. Talk about embarrassing. Dad kept slapping me on the back—all this man-to-man stuff—and saying I looked all grown up. Lois was okay. Sometimes I wish she was mean or ugly, so I could hate her, but she's not. She's pretty nice. She doesn't slobber on me, either. She yelled "nice to have you," then ran to yank Joey and Timmy off the baggage mover.

Joey's lots cuter this year. He has hair finally and six teeth. Timmy's still a pain. At the airport he kept licking the windows, then fingerpainting with his spit. I thought three-year-olds were supposed to be so terrific. That's what Lois promised me last year, anyway.

Dad makes me nervous. He talks to me in this weird new voice and makes dumb jokes and says "get it?" Usually I don't.

Gotta go. I'm writing this in the bathroom, the only place where there's a lock on the door and you can get away from Timmy. Did you take Meggie to the doctor yet? I bet she screamed bloody murder. I'm glad I'm not a kid anymore. Nobody's ever sticking a needle in me again.

Chow, McBride. (That's French for "see ya.")
                                        Alex

Randi smiled and stuck the wrinkled letter back in the envelope. Then she pulled out her new stationery in the shape of a triple-dip cone. She began to write on the top ice cream ball.

> *Greetings, Alexander the Great!*
>
> *Got your letter this morning. Hope you don't have to write all of them locked in the bathroom!*
>
> *You'll never guess who walked in last night—to stay. That's right. The famous writer. Mom's setting up her office right now. A private office where she can write the Great American Novel and us mortals won't disturb her. Absolutely No Trespassing!!!*
>
> *Actually, she seems happy. No matter what, I'll never trust her again, anyway. Who knows when she might decide to take another hike?*
>
> *Can I ask you something personal? How can you stand to visit your dad for the entire summer? I mean, after he walked out on you. I can hardly look at my mom without wanting to pull her hair out. I'll never forget what she did to us, especially to Meggie. I would if I could. In fact, I'd love to reach back over this whole year and wipe it out of my life. I'd give anything to make things the way they used to be.*
>
> *I wish you were here instead of Newport. I have a zillion things to tell you. Try to have fun this summer. Don't let Timmy flush all your socks this year.*
>
> *Ciao to you, too. (And it's Italian.)*
>
> *Randi*

After addressing the envelope with purple marker, Randi stamped it and walked barefoot down the cracked sidewalk to the corner mailbox. As she dropped her letter through the slot, she wished she could climb in the mailbox, too, and be shipped off somewhere.

She'd rather go anywhere but back home. Where *she* was.

Kneeling, Randi picked a dandelion growing through a crack in the sidewalk. Milky juice from the stem ran down her fingers. She crushed the flower into the sidewalk, leaving a yellowish stain.

Randi knew that, even if her mom did stay, things would never be the same again. No amount of wishing would make it so. Sighing, she got up and headed toward home.

4
T.C.

Randi knew no one ever lived happily ever after. So she held her breath all the next week, waiting for the ax to fall.

Only it didn't. Having her mother back home was like having a well-mannered guest around. She showed up for meals, but spent the rest of her days in her office. When Randi listened at her door, sometimes she heard typing, sometimes muttering, but often nothing at all.

It was irritating the way her mom hid in her office. Like walking on eggshells, Randi found herself tiptoeing around her own house, afraid to disturb her mother in case genius was burning.

Mostly, though, she hurt for Meggie. Several times a day Randi found her outside the office door, clutching that yellow head scarf and sucking her thumb. Meggie hadn't sucked her thumb in months. Having her mom home, but practically untouchable, was harder on Meggie than being alone. Angrily, Randi wondered why her mom had bothered to come home at all.

Early Friday morning, when her mother had been home a full week, Randi realized she'd forgotten something. "After you make your bed, come downstairs with me," she told Meggie. "It's been too long since T.C. had his litter box changed."

"Okay." Meggie threw her bed together and pounded down the lumps. "I'm ready."

As they neared the office door, muffled sounds of typing could be heard. They tiptoed past, through the kitchen, and down to the basement. T.C., Meggie's yellow-and-white cat, bounded from his home in the corner.

"P.U." Randi pinched her nose. "Better get that new bag of litter while I go dump this outside."

Five minutes later, Randi was back with the emptied box. Smiling, she watched Meggie clean T.C.'s fur with a doll brush. The cat squirmed, but Meggie was gentle. "There, now. You look so much better," she crooned. "Not like something the cat dragged in." Meggie giggled. "That's what Daddy always says."

She was crouched down in front of the half-finished two-story dollhouse their dad had started last winter. It had been intended as a Christmas present for Meggie, but he had never finished it.

Like a lot of things, Randi thought, shaking her head. Like the half-spaded flower beds out front that never got planted this spring. Or the half-painted house, brown on two sides and green on the others. No matter how much enthusiasm her dad started with, they could never depend on him to finish a project. *Oh, well*, she thought, *at least he'd never run out on them.*

"Hey, where is everybody?" Their mom's voice sounded faintly irritated.

31

"Downstairs," Randi yelled back.

Meggie squatted on her haunches, cradling T.C. in her arms like a baby, the yellow scarf wrapped around him. Her face lit up as their mother came down the stairs.

"*Whew!* Sure smells down here," she said, perching on the bottom step after dusting it off.

"I forgot to change the litter box on time," Randi muttered, mad for giving her mom a reason to criticize. She poured the bag of litter into the old plastic dishpan that served as a box, then put it near the dollhouse, where T.C. slept on a pile of old rags.

Meggie skipped over to the stairs with her cat. "Look, Mommy! This is T.C."

"T.C.? What do the letters stand for?"

"Two Colors. See? He's yellow and white." She proudly held out the purring cat.

"Two Colors? I'd have thought any child of mine would be a trifle more creative." She laughed, then stopped short at Randi's glare. "I'm sure he's a nice cat, but what was your father thinking of to let him live in the house? He smells, and no doubt there's cat hair all over. So . . . unsanitary."

Randi broke in. "T.C.'s a good cat. Meggie got him in October. I'm surprised she didn't tell you. Anyway, we couldn't put a little kitten outdoors in the snow."

Meggie leaned against her mother's leg. "T.C.'s so smart. He thinks up jokes and riddles and tells them to me."

Randi rubbed the cat's stomach. "What joke did T.C. tell you today?"

Meggie sat up tall and took a deep breath. Speaking slowly and carefully, she asked, "What do you call a rabbit with lots of fleas?"

"I don't know," Randi said. "What *do* you call a rabbit with lots of fleas?"

"*Bugs Bunny!*"

Randi fell backward laughing, although she had heard Meggie's joke at least five times already. "That T.C.! What a smart cat."

Meggie kissed the cat's nose. "Sure is a good thing I can understand what he says."

"Now, Miranda, you know Megan can't possibly—"

"By the way, Meggie," Randi spoke up quickly, "you'd better run upstairs and get his milk. T.C. looks pretty hungry."

"Okay." Meggie handed the cat to Randi, then clomped up the wooden steps. "I'll warm it up in the microwave, too. He always likes that."

When the door at the top of the stairs closed, Marilyn snapped, "I don't appreciate being interrupted like that. And I don't want you to encourage Megan in this ridiculous fantasy about a cat that tells jokes."

Randi backed off, carrying T.C. "It's a harmless fantasy."

"She must hear the jokes on TV."

"So? What does it hurt to let her make believe?"

Her mother's voice was hard. "Megan's five years old. It's about time she outgrew her fantasies." She stood up stiffly. "Life is no picnic. The sooner she learns to cope in the real world, the better."

Randi glared at her mother's back as she retreated up the stairs. She agreed with her on one point—real life *was* no picnic.

Still, who was *she* to criticize Meggie's make-believe world? Marilyn was thirty-three years old, and she hadn't coped with reality too well herself. In fact, she'd run away from it for an entire year.

Maybe Meggie *was* hanging onto some babyish ideas, but Randi intended to let her. T.C. was necessary for Meggie's well-being. He didn't just tell jokes. More than once Randi had stood at the top of the basement stairs and overheard Meggie telling T.C. that "Mommy's coming back soon," that "Mommy still loves Meggie," and "everybody will be happy again." T.C. filled an empty place in Meggie's heart, and Randi wouldn't let anyone rip that away from her.

An hour later Randi heard the clunk of the mailbox, but her mother beat her to the door again. Randi wondered what was suddenly so important about the mail.

"Another letter from Alex?" her mom asked, tapping it with a long fingernail. "It's only been a week since his *last* letter. Something going on between you two that I should know about? What is he? Fourteen or fifteen by now?"

"We're just friends." Randi snatched the letter and turned away.

"Hold it a minute. Here's a doctor bill for some tests for Megan." She waved the paper in the air. "Why didn't anyone tell me she was sick last week?"

"Drat it," Randi muttered. The bill reminded her that she had forgotten to mail in the TB test postcard four days ago. She would check Meggie's arm right away for bumps.

"I asked you a question. Why didn't you tell me Megan was sick?" her mom demanded. "I have a right to know. I'm her mother, remember. Not you."

You haven't acted much like a mother lately! Randi screamed inwardly. Outwardly, she spoke quietly. "Meggie wasn't sick. I took her in for her kindergarten checkup and booster shot. She can't register for school without them."

"I know that," Mrs. McBride said almost guiltily. "I'd forgotten, that's all."

Feeling smug, Randi enjoyed her mother's embarrassment. Well, Randi thought, she *ought* to feel guilty for not being there when Meggie needed her.

"Um . . . did Megan cry at Dr. Benoit's? I know she's always hated shots."

Randi stared for a long time before she answered. "No, she didn't cry. This past year, she's grown up a lot. She's had to."

Leaving her mom to stare at the doctor's bill, Randi fled to her room with Alex's letter. She was amazed to hear from him again so soon. He must have answered her letter the minute he got it.

Locking the door, she ripped the envelope open.

Wow, McBride! Your mom dropped a bombshell, didn't she? Why does all the excitement happen after I leave? Bet Meggie's glad to have her back.

You asked how I could stand to be around my dad now. I think it's because our family was different. When he left I wasn't that surprised. We used to get woken up every night by all their yelling. Even so, I resented him for not working things out with Mom.

It was different with you. I thought you had a perfect family. Your mom was always making cookies and going on field trips and being room mother. If there's no screaming or yelling, you figure everybody's happy. When your mom left, it was more of a shock.

I can see why you want to punch out your mom every time you look at her. But think about your dad and Meggie. If they're glad she's back, try not to hate her for them.

I'm not much help, am I? It's been five years now since Dad walked out on us, and I almost forget how hard it was. After your mom's been home awhile, maybe you'll start to forget, too.

To answer your question: No, Timmy hasn't

*flushed my socks yet this summer. I hide them in
my pillowcase. But he totaled my football. He put
it under the back wheel of Dad's car to see if it
would pop. It did.*

*Keep writing. Dad's acting weirder every day. I
wonder what's up. He watches me like a hawk and
it gives me the creeps. But Lois is okay. Seems funny
to have someone who's twenty-six for a stepmother.
She's closer to my age than Dad's!*

*Hope things go okay for you. Give your mom a
chance.*

Alex

Randi threw the letter on the floor. Give her mom a
chance? She hardly deserved that. Alex was right—he *had*
forgotten how it felt. Still, he had a point. Meggie and
her dad were glad to have her mom back, and Randi didn't
want to spoil things for them.

Flopping down in her green bean-bag chair, Randi
punched at a tiny hole until some white beads squished
out. She tossed them across the room, then balanced her
writing board on her lap and began:

Dear Alex,

*I can't believe you wrote again so soon. Things
are still the same here, even with Mom back. I still
do all the work I did all year. Her Highness doesn't
come out of her office until the chores are done.*

*But Meggie and Dad are happier. I think they're
already forgetting what this year was like. I can't
forget, though, and I don't want to. I don't intend
to forget or let her forget, either. In some way, I'm
going to make her pay for what she did to us. I'm
not five years old like Meggie and so easy to fool.
Anyway, I don't need a mother anymore.*

Sorry your dad is acting strange. And parents think kids are the problem!!! Too bad about your football. Can't your dad buy you another one? I sure am glad Meggie's not that awful age anymore. (T.C. the Talking Joke Cat is lots easier to put up with.)

Two weeks ago, I couldn't wait for school to be out for summer vacation. Now I can't wait for school to start again, so I can get away from Mom during the day. You never win, do you?

Take it easy.

Randi

She sealed the envelope, then slipped on her thongs and padded down to the corner mailbox with her letter. If only Alex were home, Randi sighed. She missed having someone she could be honest with, somebody who didn't act shocked, no matter what she said.

Heading back up her sloping driveway, Randi thought she saw the curtains flutter at her mom's office window. Was she being watched?

In case she was, Randi pasted a smile on her face and skipped lightly through Meggie's hopscotch drawn on the sidewalk. Then she bent to pick three white clover, closing her eyes as she inhaled the delicate fragrance. No matter what, she intended to look like someone who didn't have a care in the world. Her mother would never see how much she was bleeding inside.

And it all had been so unnecessary. That was the hardest part to understand. There *hadn't* been noisy fights between her parents, like at Alex's house. No one had forced her mother to leave. Her mom had had no right to think only of herself, to hurt them all when none of them deserved it.

Randi leaned against the screen door and rubbed her

forehead wearily. What about Meggie? She was so young. Who knew what permanent damage had been done to her? And all because her mother had to "find herself."

Well, Randi decided, she would have to make the best of things. Her mom and Meggie would grow close again, and probably her parents would patch things up. But one thing Randi knew for sure—she would keep her mom at a distance, no matter what.

She would never let herself get hurt like that again.

5

MINT DREAMS

On Saturday morning Randi was lazily flipping cookbook pages when the phone rang. Yawning, she got it on its third ring. "Hello?"

"Randi? It's Teri. Want to go swimming this afternoon? We could pick you up right after lunch."

Randi's hopes soared for a moment, then fell with a thud. "I can't. Dad had to work today after all. They're doing some kind of inventory at the store."

"Well, just bring Meggie, too. I'll help baby-sit her."

Randi heard quiet footsteps behind her and turned to see her mom in the doorway. She had one eyebrow raised in question.

Clearing her throat, Randi spoke louder. "I don't think I'd better. Remember last time? We ended up stuck in the baby pool the whole afternoon. Meggie's still afraid of deep water."

Her mom tiptoed into the kitchen and whispered, "I'll be home all day and can watch—"

39

Randi cut her off. "Sorry, Teri. I can go next Saturday, if Dad doesn't have to work." She turned her back to her mom. "Maybe you can ask somebody else. Anyway, have a good time."

"Why did you do that?" her mom asked when she hung up.

"Do what?"

"Skip the swimming. Now that I'm home, I could watch Megan. I *am* her mother, you know."

Randi bit off the words on the tip of her tongue. *Today* she remembered that she was Meggie's mother, but that was hard to count on. She'd forgotten quickly enough last year when she walked out.

Silence and resentment filled the kitchen. Her hands shaking, Randi opened a cupboard door and carefully straightened all the cereal boxes, lining them up from tallest to shortest. Finally she closed the door and pointed to a recipe. "I promised Meggie we'd make snickerdoodles today. She's counting on me. I don't like to let her down."

"Like *I* do?" her mom demanded, her dark eyes flashing.

"I didn't say that."

"But it's what you meant." Her mother's red lipstick seemed to make a sharp slash across her pinched mouth. "If you ever made any effort to understand my position, to meet me halfway. . . . But no, you stand there, so holier-than-thou, so perfect."

Randi hunched over the cookbook, her shoulders shaking. She didn't trust herself to speak. The last thing she wanted was a shouting match with her mother. Meggie was right downstairs with T.C. and would hear them. She didn't care about her mother's feelings, but a fight would upset Meggie horribly.

Taking three shuddering breaths, Randi began to gather flour, sugar, eggs, and butter for the cookies. "I'm sorry it looks that way." Her voice was calm and quiet, although she felt her mouth quiver. "I'm used to looking out for Meggie now. It's gotten to be a habit."

Her mom sniffled. "I'm sorry, too. I didn't mean that. It's just that, well, I don't know exactly how I fit into the family anymore."

You don't fit in at all! Randi wanted to scream. Instead, she went to call her sister. When she opened the basement door, strains of a lullaby drifted up to the kitchen.

" 'Hush, little baby, don't say a word, Mama's gonna buy you a mockingbird. If that mockingbird don't sing, Mama's gonna buy you a diamond ring.' "

Pausing with her hand on the railing, Randi recognized the song as one her mom used to sing to Meggie at night.

" 'If that diamond ring turns brass, Mama's gonna buy you a looking glass. If that looking glass gets broke. . . .' "

Randi crept down the steps until she could see. Meggie sat in an old rocker, holding T.C., who was wrapped in the yellow head scarf. Rocking slower and slower, she finished the song and gave T.C. a hug.

Meggie's voice was barely a whisper. "It's okay, T.C. I'll never leave you, so don't you worry. Meggie loves T.C. Meggie won't ever run away."

Swallowing hard, Randi waited a moment, then called out, "I'm ready to make those snickerdoodles now. Wash your hands, and we'll get started."

"Oh, good! I'm coming!" Meggie brushed T.C. off her lap and bounded from the chair.

Randi didn't notice when her mother had drifted back to her office, but by the time she and Meggie had mixed the cookie dough, she was gone. Methodically, Randi rolled golden dough into one ball after another, thinking that she probably should feel guilty about hurting her mom's feelings. But she didn't.

How guilty had her mom felt when she had left them? Hardly at all, from what Randi had seen. She had only come back to visit four times in the whole year. As far as she was concerned, her mom didn't deserve to slip smoothly back into the family. Oh, it would happen eventually, Randi supposed. She just had no intention of making it easy for her.

Randi and Meggie soon had the balls of dough coated with cinnamon and sugar. Meggie sat at the kitchen table, rolling her finger in the leftover cinnamon and sugar, then licking it off. While they were baking the first pans, their mother appeared in the kitchen, her monogrammed purse slung over one shoulder.

"Where're you going?" Meggie asked.

"Just over to Stella's to get the rest of my things. I didn't bring everything home with me last week."

Meggie jumped up from the chair. "Are you, I mean, well. . . . You *are* coming back, aren't you?" She clenched and unclenched her fists.

Marilyn McBride's face softened. "Of course, honey. I won't be gone more than an hour or two." She gave her a squeeze. "Maybe when I get back, we could have a little tea party with the cookies. Would you like that?"

"Could we eat the cookies outside on a blanket?"

"Sure, it'll be like a picnic." She fished her car keys out of her bag. "I'll be back soon." Then she was gone.

During an early lunch, which Meggie ate in front of Saturday-morning cartoons, Randi baked the rest of the snickerdoodles and read the morning newspaper. She was surprised to see "Back to School" ads already. It was only the middle of June. There were pages and pages, color advertisements for everything from jackets and shoes to lunch boxes and notebooks. She nodded and snapped her fingers.

"Meggie, come here!" When her sister skipped into the kitchen, Randi said, "Look here. The animal bookbag you wanted is on sale."

"Really? Can we go get one?" Meggie stuffed a snicker-doodle into her mouth.

"Yup, we should, before they're all sold out. We could get some other things you'll need at the same time."

"Let's go now! I love to ride the bus!" she cried, crumbs spewing across the paper.

"Okay. Just let me get some money." Randi reached to the back of the kitchen drawer, under a file box, where she kept the money her dad gave her every week for household expenses. Almost thirty dollars was left in the envelope. She folded the bills and stuffed them down in the bottom of her purse.

By the time they arrived at the bus stop, their mom had been gone over an hour. Waiting on the cement bench, Randi watched the corner anxiously. They had to be gone before her mother got home.

Randi shook her head at the rumbling in her stomach. Why did she have to feel guilty for taking Meggie shopping, anyway? She wasn't doing anything wrong, for pete's sake. There were things Meggie needed for school, and it was smart to shop before they got picked over.

Even so, a little voice in the back of her head kept reminding her about the tea party Meggie and her mom had planned. Randi wasn't kidding herself. Even though she *did* want to get Meggie that bookbag, mostly she wanted to ruin her mom's plans and be gone when she got back. At least she'd make her mom wait a good long while.

Grimly, Randi pushed her twinge of guilt down, ignoring it. *I'm not doing anything wrong,* she reminded herself. *And I'll make Meggie happy at the same time.*

With a sigh of relief, she spotted the bus round the corner and head for their stop. She pulled her wrinkled bus ticket from her pocket and took Meggie's hand.

Three long hours later, Randi half-carried her sleepy sister back off the bus, where she had dozed most of the way home. Juggling assorted packages in one arm, she held onto Meggie with her other hand.

"Come on. We're almost home," Randi said. "Pick up your feet a little."

Randi's arms ached from lugging the sacks and boxes around the mall and over to the Dairy Sweete, where they had stopped for hot fudge sundaes before coming home. Randi was already sorry about that. Her stomach had been churning before, and the ice cream hadn't helped.

When they reached the back door, it flew open before Randi could touch the doorknob.

"*Where* have you both been?" their mother demanded. "I've been worried sick for two hours!"

Head high, Randi squeezed past her mother and dropped the packages on the kitchen table. "We went shopping at the mall. They had some great school sales."

"*What?*"

Meggie rummaged through the sacks and pulled out her new cat-shaped bookbag. "Look, Mommy! Isn't this neat? The lady at the store even sewed my name on it." She held it up proudly. MEGGIE was stitched across the top flap.

"That's very nice, Megan," Marilyn McBride said, her words clipped. "I wish your proper name could have been sewn on. Why don't you take it to your room?"

"Okay." Meggie skipped off, swinging the bookbag by the long straps.

"What else did you buy?" Her mother's voice was icy.

"Just school stuff. Notebooks and folders for me, a fall jacket on sale for Meggie. I bought it a size too big, so she'll be able to wear it at least two years."

Her mom nodded, but said nothing.

Flustered, Randi dropped her gaze. "Let's see, I got her some underwear, too, and socks she needed, and new barrettes for the first day of school. They're shaped like little rollerskates," she added quietly, her confidence running down.

"Where did you get the money for all this?"

"Dad gives me money every week for household expenses. I used that."

"I see." Although she spoke calmly enough, Randi could tell her mom was furious. Two pinched white lines dented the corners of her mouth. "I have one more question: Why didn't you leave me a note so I wouldn't worry about you?"

"I guess I got out of the habit of leaving notes while you were gone," Randi said, peeling green price stickers from her folders. "I never thought about it."

"Well, in the future, please think about it."

Just then Meggie skipped back into the kitchen to try on her new jacket. While she strutted back and forth to model it, Randi casually reached into the cupboard for two antacids. She had taken them in the past. She hoped they worked this time—her stomach was tied in giant knots.

Her mother clapped as Meggie did one last twirl. "You look lovely. Better hang it up now, so it stays looking nice for school. Then let's have those cookies in the backyard."

Meggie unzipped her jacket. "Maybe later." She rubbed her rounded stomach. "Randi took me for ice cream before we came home, and I'm stuffed."

Her mom raised her eyebrows. "Really? Wasn't that . . . *nice* of Miranda!"

Randi scooped up the sacks to take to their room. She was glad she'd spoiled her mom's plans with Meggie. It served her right. Still, as she leaned against the bedroom door, she couldn't shake the guilty feeling in the back of her mind.

It isn't like me to be so sneaky and mean, Randi thought.

Look what she's done to me. I never wanted it to be this way. If only she hadn't run off, we could have been really close, I bet.

Flopping onto her bed, Randi kicked off her dusty sandals. Surely her stomach would calm down soon. She just hoped she wasn't coming down with a flu bug of some kind.

The antacids worked, though, and Randi felt better that evening. After her shower, she was more relaxed than she had been since her mother's return. Maybe if she went to bed early with a good book, she could stay relaxed and then fall asleep. She hadn't slept well in a week.

Padding back to the bedroom, she found Meggie jumping on her bed. "Look what's on your dresser! Daddy said they're a surprise."

Sitting beside her lamp were two Russell Stover Mint Dreams, Randi's favorite candy in the world. The huge chocolates were filled with a creamy mint center. Her mouth watered. She hadn't had a Mint Dream in weeks. Even if she had to brush her teeth again, she'd devour them both tonight.

Padding back down the hall, she started to poke her head into her parents' bedroom. The door was only partly closed, but her dad's voice came through clearly. She raised her hand to knock, but his words caught her off guard.

"I know, Jim, I know, but sales are always slow this time of year. You know that. . . . Well, yes, but I *have* put in extra hours. It just hasn't paid off yet, but it will. You'll see!"

Randi held her breath and wondered how long her dad had been on the phone. Jim was his boss, and it sounded as if there was trouble.

"I come on too strong with customers? You mean I'm pushy?" her dad said. "Maybe. I hadn't noticed. . . . Sure, Jim, I've just had my mind on other things lately."

Gritting her teeth, Randi knew what her dad was talking about. Everyone was under a lot of strain since her mom came home. Evidently it was affecting his work at the store.

"No, of course not. I know everyone has to pull his own weight. I'm just in a temporary slump, that's all."

Randi chewed her lip. Her dad's sales must be way down. Last year, just before her mom left, he'd won a deluxe microwave oven for being the district's top man.

Realizing her hands were clammy, Randi wiped them on her pajamas. She waited until her dad hung up, then counted to ten and pushed the door open. "Thanks for the candy, Dad. It's my favorite kind." She blew him a kiss.

He turned from where he sat on the bed, his hand still on the phone. "I've seen you drooling at the candy counter in the drugstore," he said. "Now, me, I like those chewy toffee kind. I could eat those all day. Now that's an idea! Maybe I could give out free toffee with every washer-dryer combo I sell! What do you think?" His laughter sounded forced.

"Anything's worth a try. Well, thanks for the candy."

"I can't take credit for it, actually. Your mother picked them up on her way back from Stella's today. She remembered you liked them."

Randi's eyes narrowed suspiciously. "Really?" she asked. As she stared at the minty green paper on the candy, it suddenly didn't look so good anymore.

Wearily she trudged back to her room. In the other bed Meggie slept deeply. Very slowly, Randi peeled the sticky wrappers from the Mint Dreams, then dropped the candy into the wastebasket. Was her mother trying to buy her love with candy? She really had a lot of nerve. Meggie was a nervous wreck, her own stomach was a mess, and her dad's job was in trouble. Did Marilyn think abandoning them for a whole year could be repaired with eighty cents' worth of chocolate?

Not a chance, Randi thought. *Not a chance.*

She was in bed reading an hour later when her dad ducked in to say good night. After a quick kiss, he started to leave, but halted beside her wastebasket. He stared into it for several seconds before speaking. Randi clenched her fists underneath her sheet.

"What's this candy doing in the garbage? Was it moldy or something?"

"No, not exactly." Randi scrunched down farther in bed.

"What do you mean, not exactly?"

"Well, I think I'm allergic to those Mint Dreams now. They make my stomach hurt. Too much sugar, I guess." Randi hoped she sounded convincing.

"That's odd." Her dad came back to stand by her bed. "You didn't mention it earlier. Of course, that was before you knew your mother had bought them."

"That has nothing to do with it," Randi said defensively. "I just don't like Mint Dreams anymore."

Mr. McBride paced back and forth across her bedroom. "You've simply got to accept that your mother's home for good. You're holding her at arm's length, and she feels it."

Randi sat forward abruptly, stung by his words. "Has she been complaining about me? You should know that *I'm* the one who still does all the cooking and cleaning around here. She hardly lifts a finger." Randi lowered her voice at her dad's frantic glance toward the door.

"Shh! I'm not talking about that, and I think you know it." He picked up the new notebooks stacked on her desk. "Your mom told me about the shopping trip."

Randi opened her mouth to protest, but could tell by

her dad's disappointed expression that he'd guessed her real reason for going. Her jaw snapped shut.

"Trying to keep her from feeling like part of the family isn't going to accomplish anything." His trim body sagged as he leaned forward. "It just makes you look rude."

"Rude?" Randi threw Muddy down on the floor. "*Rude?* If Mom got what she deserves, it would be a lot worse than rudeness. Anyway, I'm just treating her the way she's treated me all year."

"I don't remember her being rude to you."

"What else would you call it? Remember the times I called Stella's apartment to talk to Mom? Mom was always too busy 'creating.' Stella said she didn't want to be disturbed and would call me back later." Randi clutched her cramping stomach. "She hardly ever called back, though. And you call *me* rude?"

Mike McBride rubbed his hands together, back and forth, as if trying to warm them. "I know it's been a horrible year for you. It was for me, too, but can't we put it behind us now?" He pushed his blond hair back from his forehead. "Couldn't you try to patch things up with your mother?"

Randi studied her dad's face. With a sinking feeling, she saw that he really wasn't concerned about her feelings at all. He wanted peace at any price. Regardless of how hurt she felt, he wanted her to pretend a love she didn't feel and smooth things over.

"I'll try," she finally mumbled.

"Good." Her dad patted her leg. "Good! No reason we can't be one big, happy family again!" Smiling, he left.

Randi fell back on her pillow, exhausted. Patch things up? How? If only she had some magical Band-Aids, ones that would cover all the old hurts, all the bruised places inside.

Since she didn't, she reached under her pillow for two

more antacids. Popping them into her mouth, she chewed the chalky pink tablets.

Although she still couldn't forgive her mother, maybe she had better *look* as if she had. Her mom's feelings didn't matter much to her, but she didn't want her dad and Meggie to be more upset. She could at least do that much for them.

6

■

CONFRONTATION

The following week, Randi tried to keep in mind her dad's request to "patch things up." She had always wondered how it felt to be an actress. Now she was having plenty of chances to find out.

One morning her mom suggested they make new curtains for Randi's bedroom. Randi had forced her face into a smile and spent two afternoons learning to run the sewing machine. Later, when her dad suggested a family Monopoly game, Randi agreed and even made the popcorn. No one noticed—or cared to notice—that her enthusiasm was all an act.

By the end of the week, however, Randi admitted to herself that the playacting was a real strain. The constant fake smiling made her stomach churn even worse. In addition to the antacids before bedtime, she often woke in the night to reach under her pillow for more.

When she dragged herself out of bed Saturday morning, Randi wondered how she could possibly last until school started. She wasn't sure, at that point, if she'd even make it through June! Although she held it back, the anger inside felt like a volcano waiting to erupt.

At breakfast her dad smiled and flexed his muscles for her. "Want to go down to the hardware store with me? I need more paint to finish the house. You know how I love to keep things looking nice."

Randi jumped at the chance to get away from her mom for a while. "Sure! I'll run and comb my hair. I can be ready in two minutes." A minute later she was back. "You coming, too, Meggie?"

"Nope. I don't want to miss 'Bears in Outer Space.' I love that show."

"Okay. See ya," Randi said, relieved. If Meggie stayed home, that meant her mother would, too.

The next hour was far from thrilling, but Randi was able to relax a little. It was great being with her dad, not having to weigh every word before she spoke. She even enjoyed watching the salesman mix and shake the paint cans, although she doubted her dad would paint more than a few boards before quitting.

She helped him carry the gallon paint cans into the garage when they got home. "When are you going to start?" she asked.

"Oh, after lunch, I think." Mike stretched, his rippling muscles showing evidence of regular workouts at the Y's gym.

"It might be hot after lunch," Randi said, hiding her smile.

"You're right. I'll start this evening when the sun's almost down. With the outside lights, I'll still be able to see, and it'll be much cooler."

"Good idea." Randi chuckled inwardly, suspecting that when night finally came, it would be too damp, chilly, or mosquito-y to paint. She quickly lined up all his paint-brushes from biggest to smallest, then followed him inside.

In the kitchen, Randi paused at the telephone. A note was stuck to the bulletin board on the wall. *"Miranda—baby-sit tonight, 7:00, Jacobsens,"* her mother had scrawled.

Randi ripped the note from the board and marched down the hall. Irregular typing trickled out from her mom's office. Randi tapped on the door lightly and opened it far enough to poke her head through.

"When did Mrs. Jacobsen call?"

"Half an hour ago." Her mom didn't look up from the typewriter.

"Am I supposed to call her back?"

Marilyn McBride twisted around in her padded vinyl typing chair. "You don't need to. I told her you'd be there."

"You *what?*" Randi demanded.

Her mom blinked several times in surprise. "I told her you weren't busy. Did I forget some plans you've already made?"

Randi came in and shut the door firmly behind her. "No, I haven't made any other plans. That's not the point."

"Then what *is* the point?" her mom asked, sounding irritated. "You act as though I've committed the unpardon-able sin, when all I did was accept a baby-sitting job for you. What's the big deal?"

Randi leaned against the door as waves of nausea washed over her. She gripped the cold metal knob that pressed into her back. Breathing deeply, she tried to keep her dad's words in mind.

Her mom tapped a stack of papers on her desk. "Look, either tell me what's the matter, or clear out. I'm working on a new book—which is hard enough without interrup-tions—and I'd like to get back to it."

Randi's head jerked up. "Okay, I'll tell you what's wrong.

You had no right to tell the Jacobsens I'd baby-sit. Not without asking me first. I make my *own* decisions. I managed just fine the whole year you were gone."

"So you keep reminding me." With a tiny bristled brush, her mom absentmindedly cleaned her typewriter keys. "I told Mrs. Jacobsen yes because I thought you loved kids. I see how good you are with Megan."

"That has nothing to do with it!" With difficulty, Randi lowered her voice. She didn't want Meggie or her dad to hear them. "You're right about one thing—I do love kids. More than *some* people I could name."

"Meaning?" Her mom sounded bored as she picked out the clogged keys with a toothpick.

Her tone of voice infuriated Randi. "Meaning that *I* would never go off and leave kids that I said I loved." Randi faltered at her mom's stunned expression, but then plunged on. "You deserted Meggie and Dad, for no good reason."

"I had my reasons. Anyway, it's obvious they got along fine while I was gone." She turned her back on Randi, inserting fresh paper in the typewriter. "It was just something I had to do—for me. You're too young to understand. Anyway, I don't have to make excuses to you."

Flabbergasted, Randi gripped the doorknob to keep her knees from buckling. She couldn't believe her ears! Her mom didn't sound the least bit sorry, as if she'd done nothing wrong at all when she left. What more was there to say?

Randi turned to leave. The door was half open when her mom's voice stopped her.

"Miranda, do you . . . hate me?" Her voice was barely more than a whisper.

Randi gasped. What a question! Of course she didn't hate her mom. Only really rotten people hated their parents.

"No, of course not." Randi stared at the golden wood grain of the door. "I'm just tired. I didn't sleep too well last night."

She slipped out and pulled the door closed behind her. Doubling over, sharp stomach pains took her breath away. Biting her lip, she crept to her room and crawled into bed. Under the pillow, she found two antacids in their cellophane package. She was startled to note that there were only three left in the box by the bed.

Curled up into a ball, Randi tried to relax, but the spasms got worse. Moaning, she sneaked across the hall to the bathroom for the hot-water bottle. She filled it from the faucet, then went back to bed and pressed it against her stomach.

Her mother's question—"Do you hate me?"—forced her to take an honest look at her feelings. Squirming inwardly, Randi didn't much like what she saw. She had to admit that if she didn't actually hate her mother, the ugly feeling was something awfully close. Contrary to what she'd told her dad, she honestly didn't want the situation with her mother to get any better. Randi gritted her teeth. In fact, if she could, she'd make her mom feel as rotten as she felt.

And yet . . . Randi knew she loved her mother very much and always would. *This is insane,* she thought. *How can love and hate for someone live inside the same person?* The love she felt for her mother drew them together, while at the same time the hate was pulling them apart.

Still, her mom deserved it, even if she wouldn't admit she was guilty of anything. She had hurt them all, and it hadn't been necessary, no matter how much she talked of "finding herself."

Hugging her ragged stuffed monkey, Randi pushed the thoughts from her mind. Thinking about it never did any good—there was no simple solution.

When she woke up from her nap half an hour later, Meggie was standing three inches from her face. "This letter came for you. Can I open it?"

"Sorry, squirt." Randi yawned and grabbed the letter from Alex. She dropped the water bottle on the floor, relieved that her stomach was no longer in knots. She settled back on her pillow to read.

> *Find a place to hide, McBride! The parents are going bananas!*
>
> *Wish I could come home. For a switch, the boys aren't bad—it's my dad who's driving me crazy. I don't know what's wrong with him.*
>
> *Like last night. He's been lifting weights in a fancy gym he set up in the basement. He came up to the living room after working out and challenged me to some arm wrestling. I figured, what the heck? I'm in pretty good shape. So we arm wrestled awhile. He's strong, but I beat him the first two times. You should have seen him! He jumped up, all red in the face, and yelled at Lois for watching.*
>
> *Then he challenged me to a race around the block. He's been jogging, too, in the mornings before work. I didn't want to. Who wants to look like a fool in front of the neighbors? That made him even madder. He yelled something about "youth being wasted on the young" and stomped out of the room.*
>
> *I don't know what's happened to him this last year, but he's making me crazy. Speaking of crazy, how's your mom doing? Bet she's changed since last year. (And I thought it was us adolescents who gave everybody so much to worry about!)*
>
> *Chow, McBride. Oops! Ciao. Hang in there.*
>
> *Alex*

56

Randi shook her head. Maybe her mom wasn't so weird after all. It looked like lots of parents needed their screws tightened. No wonder she and Alex were such good friends. They had a lot in common. Chewing on the end of her pencil, she bent over her notebook.

Dear Alex,

Sorry to hear your dad's gone haywire. I wish I could help, but my dad never acted like that. He works out, but he's never challenged me to arm wrestling. Ha, ha.

You asked how Mom and I were getting along. Not at all. The first couple of weeks she was home, I was so mad that I had all this extra energy. I got so much done and hardly needed any sleep. I was going to show her that we got along just great without her.

But I ran dry this week. Suddenly I'm so pooped all the time. Maybe it's because I can't sleep anymore. And my stomach hurts again, just like it did after she left last year. No matter how much it hurts, though, I'll never let Mom know.

I'd better go. Don't race your dad around the block, no matter what he says. What if he had a heart attack or something? You don't want that on your conscience. We've got enough worries as it is.

Ciao to you, too.

Randi

She stamped her envelope and slid the letter inside, intending to mail it on the corner. At the last minute, though, she left it on the hall table to be mailed the next day. She was too exhausted to go anywhere but back to bed. Especially if she had to baby-sit that night.

Fluffing up her pillows, Randi grabbed her murder mystery. Soon she was absorbed in trying to unravel characters and clues. Half an hour later, she heard her mom come out of her office down the hall and close the door. Without warning, resentment washed over Randi again. She closed her book in disgust, knowing from past experience that she wouldn't be able to concentrate again.

She hated to admit it, even to herself, but she was getting tired of feeling mad all the time.

"Who knows?" she mumbled to Muddy. "Maybe someday I'll forgive her after all. That is, *if* she really begs me." She rubbed her cramping stomach muscles. "Maybe I won't, though," she added under her breath. "She deserves to suffer, too."

Almost unnoticed, her book slid to the floor with a thud.

7

■

MEGGIE

That night Randi piled into bed at midnight, exhausted from chasing the three Jacobsen kids all evening. An hour later a soft whimper woke her from a restless sleep. She struggled to sit up, peering across the dark bedroom. The moan came again—another of Meggie's nightmares.

"It's all right," Randi whispered as she swung her legs to the floor. "I'm coming." She had had to comfort Meggie in the middle of the night at least once a week since her mom left.

However, when she gently shook her awake, Meggie pushed her hands away and stumbled to the door. "I want Mommy," she wailed. "I want Mommy."

Randi sank to Meggie's bed as if the air had been knocked out of her. She hadn't felt so rejected in a long time. For a whole year now, Meggie had been turning to *her* when she needed something.

For sure, it was a pain sometimes to have Meggie following closer than her shadow. On the other hand, she liked feeling needed, with Meggie depending on her for everything. It was a devotion she hated to lose—especially to her mother.

"Let's go back to bed now, honey." Her mom's voice floated softly down the hall. Randi leaped into her own bed, stubbing her toe, and pulled the covers up to her chin. Soon she heard Meggie being tucked back into bed.

"There we go now. There's nothing to be frightened of." Her mother's voice was soothing. "I'll sit here until you fall asleep."

Randi forced herself to breathe deeply as her mom hummed Meggie a lullaby. Although her breathing was even, her heart raced as Randi inwardly screamed, "Trespasser! Imposter!" Her mom was such a fake. She was just playing the part of devoted mother now, for as long as it was convenient.

It was a full hour after her mother tiptoed from their bedroom before Randi fell asleep. Her stomach had churned without letting up, but she'd been afraid to make noise running water for the hot-water bottle. So, curled up in a fetal position with Muddy tucked under one arm, she drifted off at last.

Randi overslept Sunday morning, and her head ached when she dragged herself out of bed. On the way to the kitchen, she tiptoed past her parents' bedroom. Her dad's snores rose and fell rhythmically. As she passed her mom's closed office door, Meggie's giggles coming from inside stopped her in her tracks.

What was Meggie doing in there? Randi put her ear to the door. Short taps on the typewriter were punctuated by shrill little squeaks. With barely a sound, Randi turned the knob and eased the door open a few inches.

Meggie sat at the desk on her mother's lap. "Now what?" she asked, pudgy fingers poised over the keyboard.

"*D.*" Her mom paused. "Then another *D* and a *Y.*"

With another giggle, Meggie leaned over and tapped three times. "There. Does that really spell Daddy?"

"Really. What else do you want to spell?"

"Um, how about Space Cats?"

Randi watched with envy as her mom kissed the top of Meggie's head. "Space Cats it is, then. S. P. A. C. . . ."

Pulling the door closed, Randi headed back to her bedroom. She had lost her appetite. No one would notice the faucet running in the bathroom now. After filling the hot-water bottle, she crawled back into bed. She tried not to be jealous of Meggie, but it was hard. Their mom had never invited *Randi* into her office, not once. Now she felt more shut out, more lonely, than ever. Even if things were never the same with her mom, Randi had never imagined Meggie would desert her, too.

Curled around the heated water bottle, Randi recalled the night before when Meggie had run to their mom after her nightmare. It was almost as if Meggie had betrayed her. After all Randi had done for her all year, Meggie pushed her aside the minute her mom waltzed back into the house.

And how long would this cozy family last?

Suppose their mom stayed long enough to give Meggie some feeling of security, then decided they were stifling her career again. Could Meggie survive another terrible ripping apart if their mom left a second time? Randi doubted it.

There was only one thing to do. *I'll have to keep Meggie from depending too much on Mom,* Randi decided. *She can't be trusted.*

Randi reached for the new box of antacids she had sneaked from her dad's nightstand. She chewed two. After another twenty minutes her stomach still hurt, so she gave up and got dressed. More and more, stomach cramps were a part of her day. Randi wished she knew what else to do about it. Sometimes she could hardly stand up straight.

She had read about ulcers. With a gnawing fear, Randi wondered if she had one.

Her thoughts were interrupted as Meggie bounced into the bedroom. "Guess what?" she asked, waving a piece of typing paper under Randi's nose. "I learned how to spell everybody's names. Mommy showed me. I typed them on Mommy's typewriter."

Randi pushed the paper away. "That's nice, I guess, but don't expect to do that very often."

"Mommy says I can do it whenever she's not working." Meggie stuck out her tongue. "So there."

Randi blinked. Keeping Meggie from depending on their mom might not be as easy as she had first thought. She took a deep breath, reminding herself that it was for Meggie's own good.

"Do you understand why Mom left us last year?" she asked, pulling Meggie onto her bed beside her.

"Well, she wanted to write a book. And she did!"

"Do you know why she didn't write the book here? I heard her tell Dad it was because she never had any peace and quiet to work." Her mouth was suddenly dry, and she avoided Meggie's trusting gaze. "She said you interrupted her so much when I was at school that she couldn't work here. So she left."

"You mean because of me?" Meggie's lower lip quivered. "It was *my* fault Mommy went away?" Her voice rose to a wail.

"Shh! Keep your voice down." Randi hurried to shut the door. "It really wasn't your fault. Mom could have written while you napped or watched cartoons. I'm just warning you. If you keep bugging her in her office, who knows what might happen?"

Meggie stuck her thumb in her mouth. Crawling up into Randi's lap, she wrapped an arm tightly around her neck. "I won't go in her office again. I won't bother Mommy."

"That's a good idea."

Randi felt a momentary pang at the way she had reworded the truth. Her mom *had* been unable to write at home, but it wasn't just Meggie's interruptions. More than that, her mom claimed she had had too much work to do because everyone treated her like a maid.

Still, Randi reminded herself, it was crucial to keep Meggie from getting too close to their mother. They simply couldn't depend on her anymore.

Randi hugged her little sister close. "It's going to be all right. I'll always be here for you."

During the next two weeks, Randi watched in dismay as Meggie withdrew into her shell. Rather than spending more time again with Randi, she curled up for long hours outside the office door, waiting for their mother to stop working and come out. Meggie never laughed aloud and rarely smiled.

On Thursday morning, Randi searched her mind for something fun to do. "You know what? You'll be starting kindergarten in a couple of months. It's time to get you ready."

Meggie leaned back, her eyes brightening just a shade. "Now?"

"Yup. You need to learn your telephone number and address before school starts." Randi rummaged in Meggie's toy box and pulled out two old plastic telephones, a pink one and a blue one.

"What are you doing?" Meggie asked around the thumb in her mouth.

"You're going to use these toys to learn our phone number. Here, you take this one." She put the pink one on

Meggie's lap. "We'll pretend you're at school, and you forgot your bookbag. You're going to call me at home and tell me to bring it."

"But I don't know the phone number."

"That's what we're going to learn." Randi curled up on the floor beside her. "Now say after me: 656–2113. 656–2113." She waited while Meggie repeated it. "That's right. This is how to dial it."

For the next hour tinny telephone bells rang as Randi and Meggie had make-believe conversations. Once Meggie called to report that the school was on fire. Another time she said a giraffe was loose on the playground. By the end of the hour, Meggie could rattle off her phone number and dial it with confidence.

"That's great," Randi said, putting the telephones away. "Tomorrow we'll work on your address."

"Why?"

"In case you ever get lost. Then you could tell a policeman where you live, so he could bring you home." She squeezed Meggie's hand, noting that her fingernails were chewed painfully short. "There are a few other things you should know, but I'll see that you're ready for school in plenty of time."

"I love you, Randi." Meggie twirled around the room. "You're my best friend."

"I love you, too. Hey, want to go downstairs and raid the refrigerator? I know where the leftover fried chicken's hidden!"

"Okay!" Swinging her arms, Meggie trotted down the hall behind her.

Rounding the corner downstairs, they nearly collided with their mother. She was sorting through a handful of mail. "Anything for me?" Randi asked casually.

"Letter from Alex." She tossed it on the hall table.

"What's that?"

"Just a letter from my editor and a small package for me." Absentmindedly, she went past them and into her office.

In the kitchen, Randi pulled the chicken from its hiding place in the cheese keeper, wondering about her mom's letter. Guiltily, she couldn't help hoping that it was some kind of bad news. Maybe they weren't going to publish her book after all. Maybe they'd decided it was boring. Randi knew she was mean to think that way. On the other hand, it wasn't fair to have something great for her mom come out of the horrible year she'd put them all through.

A shriek of delight suddenly echoed down the hall. "It came! It came!" her mom was shouting.

Meggie jumped and dropped her chicken. Seconds later, their mother burst into the kitchen, waving a book high over her head.

"Look at this!" She thrust it under Randi's nose. "My advance copy finally came. Isn't it gorgeous?"

Having no choice, Randi stared at the cover. *Love Under Glass* by Marilyn Dickson McBride. It *was* an attractive cover, she had to admit.

"What's this Dickson? That's not your middle name." Handing the book back, Randi reached for her wing.

Her mom's airy excitement deflated. "Well, lots of authors use their maiden names instead of their middle names. I thought this sounded classier than Marilyn Sue McBride."

Meggie climbed on the chair to get a better look. "I think it's a pretty book, Mommy. When I learn to read, I'm going to read *your* book first." She hugged her mother around the waist.

"Thanks, sweetie, but you'd probably enjoy it more when you're Miranda's age." She hesitated, then said, "Would you like to read it, Miranda? They sent me two copies."

Slowly and deliberately, Randi nibbled on her chicken wing. The meat threatened to choke her.

Randi wanted to knock the book out of her mother's hand. How could her mom expect her to be pleased about it? That book was more than just someone's first novel. To Randi, it symbolized the reason her mother had ripped the family apart.

No matter how good it was, it was just another paperback romance. Had it really been worth all the grief their family had gone through during the past year? Randi hardly thought so.

She turned away from the book her mom held out and washed her hands at the sink. "I don't read romances anymore." She turned the water on full force. "Anyway, important books come out in hardcover first."

"What?" her mom said, raising her voice over the splashing water.

"Nothing." Randi dried her hands on the towel. "Leave the book there. Maybe I'll get around to reading it later." But she knew she wouldn't. Not ever.

Avoiding her mom's gaze, Randi scooped up Meggie's chicken skin and broken wishbone. She hoped no one could hear her heart pounding as she wiped the table.

"Here, Meggie, let's wash your greasy hands. And don't give that bone to T.C. He might choke on it." Randi ignored her mother as she left the kitchen. "How was your chicken?"

"Yummy." Meggie rubbed her rounded stomach. "I wish there was more left over."

"Sorry. That was it."

Randi held her little sister at the faucet while she washed up. Wincing, she wished now that she'd given Meggie *her* chicken, too. As it was, the meat had hardened into a painful lump in her stomach.

8
∎

TESTS

After Meggie went outside to play, Randi stared at the book her mother had left on the kitchen table. There was something unreal about reading *Marilyn Dickson McBride* on the cover. It didn't seem like anyone she might know.

Glancing down the hall, Randi noticed her mom's office door was still closed, but no sound came from within. Randi sighed and leaned against the table, trying to push her guilty feelings to the back of her mind. She knew she should have been more enthusiastic about the book. To her mom, it was a big deal. And yet. . . .

Picking up the book, Randi turned it over and over. *Should I feel guilty?* she thought. *No, I don't think so.*

She couldn't separate her mom's success from what this book had cost. During the past year her mom had rarely come home, even for holidays and birthdays. At the last minute she always claimed to be at a "crucial" point in her writing.

Bitterly, Randi recalled their last Thanksgiving. She and her dad had struggled to fix a turkey and all the trimmings for a traditional feast. Their mom had promised to come for dinner—their first meal together in four months. How she and her dad had sweated to make that dinner perfect!

After planning the menu weeks ahead, Randi had shopped early. She had debated on the kind of turkey to buy, finally relying on one with a little pop-up thermometer that was supposed to tell when the turkey was cooked just right.

On Thanksgiving morning, she and her dad had been up at dawn. Their excitement was just under the surface, as they hurried to get the buttered bird in the oven, mix the cranberry salad Mom loved, and peel potatoes. They'd even fixed dressing—from a box, because neither of them had felt brave enough to try the real kind.

Even Meggie had perked up that day, singing as she made turkey favors for the table out of construction paper and jumbo marshmallows. Each turkey held a tiny sign glued on a toothpick, with a family member's name on each sign. Meggie had been so proud of her original place cards.

At twelve-thirty the tension was thick in the kitchen. They had all talked and joked more than usual, and Meggie was giddy with excitement. Even though no one had spoken their thoughts, Randi knew they were all pinning high hopes on this dinner. What better time for her parents to get back together than on Thanksgiving? It would make *all* the holidays that year more special.

As one o'clock approached, Randi had run quickly down her written checklist: The turkey was done, at least according to the popped-up thermometer. The potatoes were mashed, the rolls warmed, and the tea iced. She threw the potato masher in the sink and put the carving knife on the table. Meggie had been watching at the living room window for an hour already, and Randi was ready to collapse from the heat in the kitchen. It had been worth it, though, Randi thought at the time, because everything looked fantastic. Just the sort of festive holiday meal to relax around, remembering happier times in the past, hopefully planning for the future.

It was after one o'clock before Randi allowed herself to suspect something had gone wrong. By one-thirty, however, she was sure of it. When her mother phoned to cancel at two, it was no surprise. Even now, seven months later, Randi remembered her words.

"Oh, honey, I'm so sorry!" her mom had said. "I don't know where the time went. Chapter Nine just *flowed* this morning. When I stopped a minute ago, I couldn't believe the time!" She'd paused, yawning loudly into the mouthpiece. When Randi remained silent, she added, "Why don't you all go ahead and eat without me? It would be another hour before I got there, and frankly, I'm exhausted. Writing is hard work. Maybe we can get together one night next week."

Randi didn't remember what she had answered, just that she had handed the phone to her dad. Then she had torn the turkey favor with her mom's name on it apart, bit by bit, and thrown it into the garbage.

Shaking herself slightly, Randi glanced again at the cover of *Love Under Glass*. No, she wouldn't feel guilty, she decided. The writing of this lousy book had cost them all a lot.

She tossed it down and went to get her mail. On the way to her room, she ripped open the latest letter from Alex.

You won't believe this, McBride.

Dad's gone from bad to worse. Only now it's the car, instead of arm wrestling. Since I have my permit this summer, Dad offered to let me drive to the grocery store last night. I jumped at the chance. They haven't let me drive since I got here.

Anyway, he said I drove like an old lady! He kept telling me to go faster. Once he even pushed my leg down hard on the gas. When the car lurched ahead, I almost hit a dog in the street. So on the way home Dad said he'd drive. Guess what he asked when I put on my seatbelt? "When did you turn into such a sissy?" he said.

Anyway, he rolled down the window, turned the radio way up, and peeled out of the parking lot right over the curb. I mean, he really burned rubber. I slammed my head on the side window, but he didn't even notice.

About two blocks from home a little boy ran into the street after a ball. Dad was speeding, but saw the kid in time to swerve. We hit a light pole instead.

I just bit my tongue really bad, but Dad's in the hospital. Cuts and bruises, two broken ribs, and a cracked wrist. It could have been a lot worse, though. He's supposed to come home tomorrow.

I tried to talk to Lois about him today, but I just couldn't find the right words. McBride, I think he's cracking up. He's never acted this way before.

Wish I was home. I can't believe it's only the first week of July. I don't think I can take six more weeks of this.

Ciao, McBride.

Alex

*P.S. Don't mention any of this to Mom. I'll tell
her myself, but just that he hit a pole while missing
a kid in the street. Mom has enough to worry about.*

Randi refolded the smudged pages. Alex's dad *did* sound
sick. What a mess! She would answer Alex right away.
Randi rubbed her forehead. Maybe she would rest awhile,
then write a little later when she felt better. At the moment, her stomach was tied in the worst knots she had
had so far.

Between resenting her mom and worrying about Alex,
her stomach was hardly ever *not* hurting anymore. The
thought of an ulcer seemed more and more likely. An
hour later, after the antacids and hot-water bottle had
done no good again, Randi knew it was time to get help.

Tiptoeing into the kitchen, she peeked out the window
to the backyard. Her mom and Meggie were under their
apple tree, playing some kind of catching game with the
green apples that had blown to the ground.

Good, Randi thought. *I'll have some privacy.*

She dialed the doctor's number from the emergency list
posted by the phone. "Dr. Benoit? It's Randi McBride. I
wondered if you had some free time this week." She de-
scribed her symptoms, all the while keeping a nervous
eye on the back door.

"You've done the right thing to call me," Dr. Benoit
assured her. "Let's see, tomorrow's Friday. I have a cancel-
lation at two. How about then?"

"Okay." Randi kneaded her sore stomach. "I'll be
there."

Hanging up, she reached into the back of the kitchen
drawer for the household money her dad had put there
that morning. She slipped twenty-five dollars into her
pocket to take along. Right after the appointment, she'd

pay the bill. She didn't want her mom getting another notice from the doctor and asking a lot of questions.

That night Randi slept very little, partly from the pain in her stomach, partly from worrying about what the doctor would find. The next afternoon she told her mother she was going to the library. If her mom wondered why she wasn't taking Meggie, she didn't ask.

On the way to the bus stop, she waved to Alex's mom as she pulled out of their driveway in her beat-up old Toyota. For the hundredth time, Randi wished Alex was back.

Fifteen minutes later at the doctor's office, Randi spread a magazine across her lap and pretended to read. Her stomach grew worse while she waited, yet she wished she hadn't come after all. It was probably nothing, and office calls were expensive.

"Miranda McBride. Miranda McBride." The nurse's voice twanged over the intercom.

Randi jumped, the magazine falling to the floor. Stepping around elderly patients' canes and young mothers' diaper bags, she threaded her way to the nurse.

"Dr. Benoit will be right with you," the nurse said, ushering Randi to a small examining room, then closing the door.

Randi studied the framed certificates on the wall, straightening two of them. She had the glass jars of cotton balls, tongue depressors, and disposable needles rearranged by the time Dr. Benoit breezed in. "Hello, Randi. How are you feeling today?" He combed through his reddish gray beard with his pencil.

"About the same as when I called yesterday."

"Okay. Let me ask you some questions, and then we'll have a look. First, do you notice any particular time of day that your stomach feels worse? For example, right after you wake up?"

Randi thought over the past few weeks. "No, not really. I don't think there's any real pattern."

"Does your stomach perhaps hurt more just before mealtimes?" the doctor asked. "Or other times when your stomach is empty?"

"Not really." Randy recalled some tense meals lately. "Actually, it hurts worse right *after* I eat than before."

"Hmmm. Well, that's probably a good sign." Dr. Benoit doodled little prancing dogs across his notepad.

"Why good?"

"If you had an ulcer, your stomach would probably hurt the most when it was empty. An ulcer's an open sore inside your stomach. When your stomach's empty, the stomach acids irritate the ulcer."

Randi relaxed slightly. "If it's not an ulcer, what do you think it is?"

"Since it hurts more after eating, you may have a blockage where your stomach empties into your intestine. However, I think that's quite unlikely." He doodled some more, then looked sympathetically at Randi. "At this point, though, I wonder if it isn't being caused by stress."

"Stress?"

"Yes, something that's upsetting you." He took Randi's hand and patted it. "I heard your mother's back home. This could cause the stress. It's bound to be an adjustment, even if things are going smoothly."

Randi snorted. *"Smoothly?* She turned our world upside down again."

The doctor nodded. "I suspected as much. A big change like this would be enough to cause your stomach pains." He motioned to the examining table. "Let's take a look first, though, and see exactly where it's hurting."

Ten minutes later he finished the examination. Although Randi had tried to relax, his gentle poking and prodding had hurt. "Did you find out anything?" she asked, almost afraid to know.

"Nothing definite." Dr. Benoit helped her sit up. "I'll need to run a few tests so I can rule out some things."

"What kinds of tests?" Randi asked. She couldn't wait to get home and curl up with a hot-water bottle. Maybe this time it would bring some relief.

"I'll arrange an upper GI series for you over at the hospital, to be done on an out-patient basis."

"Out patient? What's that?"

"You get an appointment just like when you come here. You don't have to check into the hospital, though."

"Will it hurt?" Randi asked, hoping she didn't sound as chicken as Meggie.

"No, you just drink a glassful of pink chalky-tasting liquid, then have your chest and stomach X-rayed every fifteen minutes or so. The whole series shouldn't take more than an hour, or maybe an hour and a half."

Randi clutched her billfold. She was relieved she probably didn't have an ulcer, but she doubted there was any blockage, either. What Dr. Ben had said about stress rang true, though, because the pain hadn't started until her mom came home.

". . . and my nurse will let you know when you're scheduled for the GI series."

"What?" Blinking, Randi pulled her mind back to the doctor's words.

"I said we'll make the appointment for you, then let you know when it is."

Randi thought quickly. "No, you don't need to. I'll have my dad make the appointment, so he can pick a day and time that he can take me." Randi knew he would never let her go to the hospital by herself, in case something really was wrong with her.

"That would be fine, too." Scratching his head, the

doctor added, "Before you leave, Janice'll draw a blood sample. A couple of things could be ruled out here in our own lab through some simple blood tests."

Randi's heart sank. She hated blood tests. "Okay," she agreed feebly.

"Call me tomorrow morning after nine. The test results should be in by then, and I'll let you know if we find anything." He patted her shoulder. "I'm fairly certain there's nothing seriously wrong, Randi. But if there is, we'll find it and treat it. You'll be feeling as good as new in no time."

Randi nodded, although she doubted she'd ever feel as good as new. On the contrary, she hadn't known a kid her age could feel so incredibly *old*.

After the blood test, Randi paid her bill in cash and headed for the library. She'd better come home with a few books to avoid suspicion, she thought. When she got home, she gratefully curled up with a mystery, her hot-water bottle hidden under her quilt.

The next morning, Randi was surprised to find her mom eating breakfast with Meggie. She had fixed whole wheat toast in all kinds of cookie cutter shapes. Some looked like rabbits, some like fish or cats. They all had raisin eyes and noses.

"Want a cat?" Meggie asked, butter smeared across one cheek. "We saved you some."

"I don't think so. I'd rather have a bagel." She pushed one down in the toaster, avoiding her mom's eyes.

"Guess what, Randi?" Meggie asked, squirming in her seat. "Mommy and me are going to the zoo today! We're even going to eat lunch there! Corn dogs!"

"Really?" Randi carried her bagel to the table.

Her mom examined her fingernails. "Would you like to come with us? We'd love to have you."

"No, I don't think so." With them out of the house,

she could call the doctor without being overheard. She reminded herself to call early—the doctor's office was only open mornings on Saturday. "I have some things to do in my room." With a start, she remembered Alex's unanswered letter. That was one thing she'd do today, for sure.

"Well, if you change your mind. . . ."

Randi steeled herself against the wistful tone in her mom's voice. "I doubt it." She finished her bagel in silence.

As soon as Meggie and Marilyn left for the zoo, Randi phoned the doctor's office. Dr. Benoit was with a patient, but he would call her right back.

While waiting, Randi washed up the dishes and gave T.C. the leftover toast. He purred his gratitude by sticking his claws through her cotton pajamas. She shook him off when the phone rang.

Taking the stairs two at a time, she answered breathlessly. "Dr. Benoit? I wondered about my blood tests."

"I have the results right here," the doctor said. "It's the good news we expected. Our tests ruled out several problems, so we'll do the GI series next."

"What if those X-rays don't show anything, either?"

"Well, the next step would probably be an ultrasound of your abdomen. Ultrasound is absolutely painless, Randi. You don't even have to swallow pink liquid or anything."

Randi wrapped the telephone cord around her finger till the end turned blue. "Won't all this cost a fortune?"

"The tests *are* expensive, but your family's insurance will cover them. There's nothing for you to worry about." Faint beeping sounded in the background. Randi heard Dr. Benoit being paged. "I have to go, Randi. Be sure to have your dad schedule that GI series right away. After that, we'll decide what to do about further tests."

"I will," Randi mumbled, knowing perfectly well she had no intention of going in for more tests. From what

Dr. Ben had said, she was sure her stomach pains were her mom's fault. Just like everything else was.

Randi busied herself around the house, watering plants and sorting magazines. Then she straightened all the books on the shelves in the living room, alphabetizing them by author. By the time she had finished, she finally had a sense of being under control again.

At noon she decided to skip lunch. She wasn't hungry enough to risk upsetting her stomach more with a meal. Finally, with a book and a handful of Meggie's animal crackers, Randi curled up on the couch. Soon the lines of print blurred, and she gave up. Her restless nights had left her exhausted. Enjoying the rare sense of peace in the house, she drifted off to sleep.

It seemed only minutes later when she was awakened by a slammed door. "Hey! Anybody home?" her dad's booming voice echoed from the kitchen.

Randi's book slid to the floor. "In here, Dad." She rubbed at her eyes.

"Where's your mom?" Her dad loosened his tie and yanked it off. "What a beast of a day—nothing but browsers. Millions of filthy kids leaving sticky fingerprints on everything." He collapsed into an easy chair and stretched his legs out in front of him. "Where did you say your mother was?"

"Mom and Meggie went to the zoo and are staying for lunch. What time is it, anyway?"

"A little after four."

Randi struggled to sit up. "I didn't know I'd slept that long. They should be back by now. I wonder what's keeping them."

Her eyes opened wide, alarmed at the thought that flitted through her mind. Were her mom and Meggie just late? Or was it something much worse? Was it possible? Would her mom run away again, only this time *taking Meggie with her?*

Randi's stomach lurched, and she pressed her clammy hands together. Her mom and Meggie had grown pretty close lately, in spite of her plan to keep them apart. Her mom wouldn't have had to kidnap Meggie, Randi realized. Her little sister would probably have gone willingly. Should she check the closets and see if Meggie's clothes were missing? She glanced across the room. By the panicked look on her dad's face she could tell the same idea had crossed his mind.

Before she could move, the back door slammed again. Randi's heart thudded with relief.

Meggie burst into the living room, waving a small purse. "Look what I got!" Covered with sparkling hearts, the miniature purse held a notepad of heart-shaped paper, five crayons, and a heart-shaped eraser.

"That's neat," Randi agreed, snapping the purse shut. "Did you have a good time?"

"Yup! We got *you* something, too!" Their mother waited quietly in the doorway. "Show her, Mommy."

Marilyn handed Randi a red-and-white paper sack, the zoo emblem circled on it in black. Aware of her dad's watchful eyes, she reluctantly pulled out a knit shirt.

It was red, Randi's favorite color. Soft to the touch, it had a rainbow on the pocket sewn on with glittering thread. Randi didn't know what to say. Awkward silence filled the room.

Her mom pointed to the label on the shirt's hem. "The saleslady in the gift shop said all the kids your age are wearing this kind. She was sure you'd like it," she added doubtfully.

Head down, Randi stared at the label. Her mom was right—it *was* a popular style. "There's only one problem," she said, handing the shirt back. "I haven't worn that size for eight months."

"Oh." Her mom stuffed the shirt back in the sack. "I didn't know that."

"How could you? You haven't exactly been around for a while." Randi bit her lip, regretting her sarcastic tone in front of her dad.

Her mother turned and left the room, clutching the zoo sack. "Marilyn," her dad called, "she didn't mean it." Without a word, Meggie trotted after her mother.

"Miranda, I could shake you till your teeth rattle," her dad hissed. "I thought you were going to patch things up. It's not your mom's fault she bought the wrong size."

"Isn't it? If she'd been home this past year where she belonged, she'd know what size I wore. *Other* mothers know these things."

Her dad jumped from his chair and almost lunged at her. "Can't you at least *try* to forgive her? We've all been hurt, not just you."

Randi's head snapped back as if she had been slapped. "Whose life changed the most? You still go to work every day, and have someone to cook and clean for you. Meggie's life changed more than yours since she had to start going to a baby-sitter during the school year."

"I know, but—"

Randi pushed on, barely hearing him. "But *I'm* the one who really got trampled on. I'm the one who had to run the house and take care of Meggie. I'm the one who gave up band and Girl Scouts and summer camp because I was needed at home."

The fight suddenly went out of her father. "I know it's been hard on you. It's hard for me, too. I can't even call home during the day anymore! I'm afraid I'll disturb her writing, or find out she's packed and gone again." He sagged beside her on the couch. "Somehow, though, we just have to forget the past."

"I'd like to, but how? I'll always remember what she did to all of us. Meggie's not the same little girl. She's nervous and eats all the time to feel better. All our holidays were ruined, we canceled our vacation last summer, and we quit going anywhere that's fun. This whole year we haven't gone bowling or rollerskating once, and we used to go all the time." She banged her fist on her knee. "I can't force myself to forgive her."

"How do you know?" her dad asked tiredly. "Have you tried?"

"Yes, I have," she answered, "but it's impossible." Grabbing her book, Randi ran to her room and locked the door. Doubled over on the bed, she tried to ease the stabbing pains in her stomach.

When was it going to stop? For a whole year, she had prayed for her mother to come home. Now that she had, it was stirring up feelings Randi had thought were dead. Squeezing her eyes tightly shut, she stroked Muddy's lumpy back, over and over, up and down.

She wouldn't have believed it was possible, but things were worse than ever now.

9

■

CRAZY QUILT

Randi shifted with the surging crowd at the mall, careful to keep strangers between her and the bookstore. Although Randi had been spying for half an hour, her mom still hadn't spotted her. It was tricky, keeping herself hidden from her mom without blocking her own view.

"Hey, look where you're going!" an old lady shouted at her.

"Oops, sorry," Randi mumbled, jumping backward off her toes.

Keeping her head down, she dodged shoppers who crowded the booths of the summer craft show. Pretending to study the Christmas decorations made from pine cones and the book ends shaped like mallard ducks, Randi watched the autograph party farther down the mall.

When her mom's book had been released in mid-July, the local book store had planned an autograph party for the first weekend of August. It coincided with the huge craft bazaar held every summer.

Her mom had been bubbling over about it during the last few weeks, but Randi had paid little attention to her. Their relationship had settled down some during the past month. They had "ceased fire" and rarely talked to each other. Still, Randi knew there hadn't been a real truce— it was more like a Cold War. Her mom would be surprised to know she was there.

The mall was elbow to elbow with shoving kids, screeching parents, and sellers frantically urging people to buy. Randi noticed that many shoppers stopped at her mom's table, set up in the bookstore doorway. Even from where she stood, Randi could read the glittery sign behind her mother's head: LOCAL AUTHOR SIGNING NEW BOOK! LOVE UNDER GLASS BY MARILYN DICKSON MCBRIDE.

Stacks of the paperback made twin pyramids on the round table, while a smaller pile sat at her mom's elbow. They weren't exactly selling like hot cakes, Randi noted with satisfaction, although she *was* signing two copies for junior high girls at the moment.

"Hi!"

Randi lurched forward and knocked against a card table full of home-made candy. Embarrassed, she quickly rearranged the jumbled packages. "Oh, hi, Nicole. What are you doing?"

"What do you think? I'm shopping." She glanced behind Randi. "Ooh, look. Fudge with pecans. Want to buy some and share it?"

The thought of that rich chocolate made Randi's already jumpy stomach roll over in protest. "No, thanks, I'm not hungry." She pointed at Nicole's armful of sacks. "What've you got there?"

"Lots of great junk. Let's see. This neat scarf, and a pair of earrings shaped like pretzels, and this!" She snatched a small bag from her larger sack. "I bought a copy of your mom's book, autographed and everything. Is it good?"

Randi shrugged. "I wouldn't know."

"You haven't read it?" Nicole popped a hand over her open mouth. "Oops! Sorry. I thought I heard she was living at home again."

Randi backed away a couple steps. "Word sure travels fast."

"My mom plays bridge with Alex's mom, and she mentioned it." When Randi didn't respond, Nicole shrugged and put the book away. "Well, see ya." With a shake of her head, she turned and moved away.

Randi sighed as she watched Nicole thread her way among the shoppers. That was one thing she hadn't counted on, but she should have guessed it would happen. Her mom's book would interest kids her age, so naturally her friends might read it and talk about it. Or even ask her what it was like living with a writer. Or—oh, no!

Last year during Book Week a children's writer had spoken at their school. She had been interesting, and the librarian said they would try to invite someone else this year. Randi shuddered. What if they asked her *mom* to come and speak? It was unthinkable.

Randi moved to peek at her mother from behind a cardboard tree sprouting hand-carved birds. Her mom still sat there, smiling rather wanly, her pen poised in case anyone swooped down on her to buy a book.

As Randi watched, however, no one did.

A few stopped by to leaf through a book, then pointed to the author sign. Most people merely walked by, however, either staring curiously or just ignoring her mom altogether. Randi glanced at the giant gold clock in the center of the mall. *Nearly two o'clock.* The autograph party had lasted for an hour already. Unless some ghost was mysteriously replenishing the books, her mom wasn't selling many. The pyramids were still neatly stacked, and the pile of books at her elbow hadn't shrunk much, either.

Randi shifted uncomfortably, cramped from hiding behind the crafts tables. Watching her mom's brave, determined smile, she felt a twinge of sympathy for her, but squelched it immediately. She would *not* feel sorry for her. In fact, it would serve her right if nobody bought her old book.

Slipping away from the bazaar booths, she melted into the crowd and headed away from the bookstore toward home.

A letter from Alex was in the mailbox when she got there. Passing the living room, she waved at her dad and Meggie, who were watching a baseball game on TV.

"Hi!" her dad boomed over the sportscaster's voice. "Did you have a nice walk?"

"It was okay."

"Guess what I did while you were gone?" He held up his paint-speckled hands. "I got a huge chunk of the house painted. What a hot job! I just came in for a minute to cool off, then I'll get right back at it. Don't want to have a heat stroke."

Randi nodded. She had heard *that* before. It would be a surprise if he painted anymore that day.

As she ripped open her letter, guilt washed over her. She had forgotten all about answering Alex's last letter, and it had been at least three weeks ago. Where had the time gone? She had been so wrapped up with her stomach problem and dealing with her mom that she had barely thought of Alex. She unfolded his letter.

> *Hey, there, McBride. How's life treating you these days?*
>
> *Only three weeks till I leave this nuthouse behind. It's like a tomb around here. After two days in the*

*hospital, Dad had to stay home for another week.
He was really quiet. Just sat in front of the TV all
day. He didn't care what he watched—half the time
it was a dumb preschool show with Timmy.*

*Then one day he dropped a bomb. He told us
he'd lost his job. After being with his company for
eighteen years, he got replaced by some young kid
straight out of college.*

*I guess that explains the jogging and arm wrestling.
He's been trying to prove how young he is. He keeps
saying that new job offers will start coming in any
day now. But he's not applying for any jobs. Except
to collect unemployment, he never goes out at all.*

*Lois smiles a lot, but her eyes are usually red.
Joey doesn't notice anything is wrong, but Timmy
crawls into bed to sleep with me now. I was already
having trouble sleeping, and a wiggly three-year-old
is no help.*

*Sorry to go on forever about this, but you're the
only one I tell this stuff to. With Mom, I just keep
saying I'm having a "wonderful time," but I'm
counting the days till I come home.*

*Forgot to ask—how are you doing now? Last letter,
you said your stomach was bothering you. I remember
when my dad first left, I felt the same way. You
have the right to hurt your mom back, that's for
sure, but you'd better give it up, kid. Hate will eat
your guts out.*

Come on, McBride, write! Ciao.

Alex

Randi refolded the letter, massaging her knotted stomach
muscles at the same time. Alex was sure right about one
thing—her feelings *were* eating her insides out. Determined

to answer Alex's letter that very afternoon, Randi placed it in the center of her desk where she would be sure to notice it. She would get to it as soon as she felt better.

Lounging in front of the TV the rest of the afternoon, Randi couldn't wait for her mom to get home and tell them about her autograph party. She just knew, from the hour she had watched, that it had been a total bomb.

She was unprepared for her mom's laughing eyes and springy step when she glided into the kitchen at four-thirty.

"I'm home!" she called, although all three of them were in the kitchen eating a snack and could see her.

"How'd the autographing go?" their dad asked.

"Really well, I think! Of course, this is just my first one, so I don't have much to compare it to." She kicked off her heels and collapsed onto a chair. "It was slow at first—just a lot of lookers—but for the last hour and a half I signed books as fast as I could write. There were only two copies unsold when I left."

"Really?" Mike patted her shoulder. "That's nice. You'll never guess how I've been slaving while you were out playing Miss Famous Writer."

Randi noticed the brief frown that crossed her mom's face. "I wasn't *playing* at being a writer. I *am* a writer."

"I know. I didn't mean. . . . Of course your work is important," Mike stammered. "What I started to say, well, I got most of the north side of the house painted while you were gone. Well, half of it. It'll be a snap to finish."

Randi's mom rummaged in the refrigerator for a chunk of cheese and an apple. "I'm starving. I was too nervous to eat much lunch, but I could eat a bear now."

"A bear?" Meggie giggled, then crawled into her mom's lap at the kitchen table. "I missed you," she added in a whisper.

"I missed you, too, sweetie." Marilyn McBride broke off a piece of cheddar for Meggie. "I had a wonderful time, though. All those people—buying books from me!" She grinned at the room in general.

Randi's stomach twisted. Without a word, she headed to her room. Stomping by her mom's open office door, she noted the neat stacks of paper beside the typewriter. Evidently the third book was going well, even though her mom hadn't heard yet if the second book she had finished would be published or not.

"It's not fair," Randi muttered. "It's not *fair!*"

Slamming her bedroom door, she paced back and forth from the desk to the window, flattening a path in the shag carpet. Nothing was fair, she thought, popping two antacids into her mouth. Absolutely *nothing.*

"Mom runs away, writes a book and sells it, and gets all this free publicity," Randi muttered to the cat in the poster above Meggie's bed. "And what do *I* get? Tons of housework, a stomach that needs X-rays and ultrasound, and no sleep at night." She flopped into her bean-bag chair. "Some trade."

Elbows on knees, Randi took a good hard look at what was happening. It was obvious that her mom was content as she got on with her life and new career. On the other hand, she herself was miserable most of the time. Randi's resentment wasn't hurting her mom much at all. Randi had to admit Alex might be right. This hate was eating *her* insides out. Something would have to give. And soon.

She crawled into bed early that night, but was awake by one A.M., her stomach cramping worse than ever. After an hour of counting sheep that jumped backward over fences, Randi gave in to her boiling thoughts.

Although she could usually push it from her mind during the day, the lonely nighttime hours were impossible. She would lie in the darkness, hour after hour, reliving the day her mom had left. Then, just like a horror movie, her mind would rerun events from the past year—birthdays and holidays her mom had missed, ignored phone calls, the week Randi had had the flu with only Meggie to take care of her. One scene after another, in living color, passed before her eyes. It always left Randi in a cold sweat, clutching her pillow to her stomach.

By five A.M. Randi lay exhausted, sick to her stomach, and thought it would be simpler just to die.

Instead, she dragged herself through an endless Sunday, pretending that nothing was wrong. That night, exhausted enough to sleep a full week, she crawled wearily into bed, only to find herself awake again in the middle of the night. Giving in to the tears that welled up, she tiptoed across the dark hall for the hot-water bottle. It did nothing for the pain, but it helped the chills she was experiencing more and more.

Light gray shadows had crept across the floor by the time she finally drifted off to sleep at dawn. Three hours later, Randi was jerked from her deep sleep by a jangling phone.

She lay still for a moment, waiting for Meggie or her mom to answer it, but the clicking of the typewriter keys didn't pause for a second. Evidently Meggie was with T.C. and couldn't hear it. Usually she ran to answer it. Randi groaned. How could anyone ignore a ringing phone? Groggily, she lurched to the living room and lifted the receiver.

"Huh?" She cleared her throat. "Hello?"

"McBrides?" a brisk voice asked.

"Yes, this is Randi."

"I'm sorry. I didn't recognize your voice. This is Dr. Benoit."

Randi sucked in her breath sharply. "Yes?" she whispered.

"When I checked with the hospital lab, they informed me you hadn't been in for your GI series yet. It's been several weeks, so why not?"

88

"Um, well . . ." Randi licked her lips nervously. "Well, actually, I've been feeling much better lately. I guess I don't need the tests after all."

There was a long pause on the other end of the line. It sounded like Dr. Ben was drumming his fingers on his desk.

"Are you sure? When you came to my office, you were in a lot of pain. These things rarely go away so quickly."

Randi forced a laugh. "I guess I'm just lucky." Suddenly she jerked around as the typing stopped. "Thanks for calling. Good-bye."

Randi hung up before he could answer, then immediately lifted the receiver off the hook. If Dr. Ben tried to call her right back, he'd get a busy signal. A minute later, when the typing resumed, Randi gently hung up the phone and tiptoed back to her bedroom.

If she had succeeded in fooling Dr. Ben, she ought to get an Oscar, she decided. Crawling back into bed, she pulled the colorful old quilt up to her shoulders.

Lying in the now sunny room, Randi absentmindedly examined the patchwork quilt Grandma Dickson had made years ago. There was no design to the quilt at all, just jagged, haphazard shapes held together with tiny perfect stitches. Her grandma had called the pattern a "crazy quilt."

It was odd, Randi thought. The old quilt was just like her life—full of crazy pieces, patched together with no design. Only there was one big difference: Randi knew her life was coming apart at the seams.

10

■

TURNING IT LOOSE

At the crack of dawn the following Thursday, Randi was jerked awake by the vacuum cleaner advancing down the hallway. She wondered groggily what the heck was going on.

"Oh, yeah, Grandma Dickson's coming today." She burrowed farther under the covers, but not before she noticed Meggie's bed was already empty. Sighing, she guessed she, too, should get up and help her mother, but she was exhausted after another nearly sleepless night.

With a groan, Randi pulled herself out of bed and into her jeans. She ought to be grateful her grandmother was coming. At least it had pried her mom out of her office to help with the housework for once. With any luck, she'd fix lunch, too.

The vacuum abruptly switched off. "Miranda! Get up now." Her mom stormed into the bedroom. "Oh, good, you're up. There are a million things to do before Grandma gets here. First I want you to dust."

"I just dusted two days ago."

"I know, but you'll have to do it again. Use that lemon polish stuff this time." She pushed back the hair that stuck to her sweaty forehead. "By the way, Dr. Benoit called a few minutes ago to see how you were—something about tests for your stomach?"

Randi ran a comb through spiky hair that resembled porcupine quills. Her heart hammering, she said, "It was a long time ago. I had the flu, but he wanted to do some tests. I got better before we got around to it."

"Oh, that's good," her mom said absentmindedly. "Better get busy. You know how Grandma inspects everything." With a sigh, she disappeared.

Randi buckled on her sandals. She had to admit her mom was right about that—Grandma Dickson was the original Mrs. Clean.

Ten minutes later, after Randi had eaten her toast over the sink, she grabbed her dust rag and can of polish. Turning, she collided with Meggie coming from the basement. She had the yellow scarf wrapped around her head and tied under her chin.

"Oh, good, you're up."

"Yeah. What's with the scarf?"

"I have a toothache—can't you see?" Meggie dropped a plastic pan on the linoleum. "Mommy said I had to take T.C. and his litter box out to the garage today. She says Grandma will think the house stinks."

"Here, I'll take the litter box. You get T.C." Randi waited while Meggie plodded back downstairs for the cat.

"You know," Meggie said breathlessly, struggling back up the steps with the wiggly cat, "T.C. doesn't want to go outside. He told me so."

"No wonder. It's a hot day to be shut up in the garage." Randi held the door open for Meggie. "Let's leave plenty of water for him."

"Hey, T.C. told me another joke this morning. Want to hear it?"

"Sure. T.C. tells great jokes."

"Okay. Here goes: What's green and noisy and *very* dangerous?"

"I don't know. What's green and noisy and very dangerous?"

"A thundering herd of pickles!"

Randi laughed dutifully at the old joke. "That's really good. T.C.'s one smart cat."

Meggie grinned; then her smile slowly faded. "You know what? Mommy says T.C. can't really tell me things." She nibbled the end of her thumb. "She says that's baby stuff."

"No, it's not." Mentally, Randi shook her fist at her mom. "I'm sure T.C. talks to you."

"You are?"

"Sure. Doesn't he tell you when he's hungry? Don't you always know when he's happy, or when he's scared?"

Meggie rubbed the two-colored cat under his chin, and he purred contentedly. "Yup. I always know when he's happy." She buried her plump face in his fur. "And he *always* tells me when he's hungry."

"See? You just understand cat language better than Mom. She can't understand T.C., but you know him better, so you know what he's saying." Randi deposited the kitty litter in the corner of the garage.

Meggie took the box of car-washing rags and made a bed for T.C. "Want me to help you dust?"

"No, that's okay. Stay here and play with T.C. I'll call you when Grandma gets here." Leaving Meggie to fan her hot cat with a folded newspaper, Randi shook her head at the half-painted house before hurrying back inside.

Even though she worked like a speed demon, a yellow cab pulled into the driveway before Randi finished wiping off the plant leaves. "Grandma's here!" she yelled. Closet doors banged shut down the hall.

"Already?" Her mom emerged from her bedroom, buttoning a clean blouse and patting her perfectly arranged hair. "Does the house look okay?"

Randi glanced around the living room. Every possible surface shone, reflecting the sunlight like a dozen mirrors.

"Looks like a magazine ad, if you want to know. But Grandma's coming to see you, not inspect the house."

Her mom didn't look convinced as she straightened her shoulders and opened the front door. "Hi, Mother!" she called a shade too brightly. "Come in out of this heat."

A slightly bent woman with a bulging shopping bag plodded up the steps.

"I wish you'd let me pick you up at the bus station. I would have been happy to." Marilyn took the woman's small straw hat. "It's been so long since you were here and everything. . . ."

Randi wondered why her mom sounded so nervous. True, she hadn't seen Grandma Dickson since she had moved back home. She supposed that could be it. Or was there something else?

The stocky older woman reared back and peered into her daughter's face. "Humph. You look the same. Figured you'd seem different."

Randi's mom shivered, then rubbed her hands together as if to warm them. "Different? Why?"

"Thought you'd be all gussied up now, like a city lady. But you still look like a housewife from a small town." She nodded with satisfaction, then turned to Randi. "How's my oldest granddaughter today?"

"Hanging in there. Was your bus trip nice?"

"Rough road, but I got a lot of knitting done. I'm working on some sweaters for Christmas already." She sank heavily into an armchair.

"How's Grandpa?" Randi asked. Grandpa always stayed behind on their Nebraska farm to "tend the livestock." Grandma came in alone on the bus, then insisted on taking a taxi to their house from the station.

Grandma surveyed the living room, inch by inch, before answering. "Oh, Grandpa's the same—no worse than most, no better than he deserves. Thumb's got a touch of arthritis again. Won't see a doctor, though." She pulled skeins of green and gold yarn from her bag. "Where's Megan this morning?"

"Still playing outside," Randi said. "I'll go get her."

Passing through the kitchen, she noticed the plastic laundry baskets still on the table. She ran them downstairs and threw some wet sheets in the dryer while she was there. Back upstairs a minute later, she was heading out the back door when angry voices stopped her.

"You *always* wanted too much! Greedy! Even when you were a little girl!" her grandma shouted.

Randi's hand froze on the door handle.

"Just because I wanted to leave the farm? Was that such a crime?" Randi's mom asked.

"We wanted to be quite a lady, didn't we? Only leaving the farm wasn't enough for you, was it? You were never satisfied."

Her mom's voice was deadly quiet. "What do you mean?"

"Look at you! You have a beautiful house, a husband who doesn't drink his paycheck away, and two pretty girls. But you ran off like a common piece of trash!"

"How dare you talk to me that way."

"I dare because I'm your mother! Someone has to talk some sense into you!" Her grandma's voice rose to a fever pitch. "You should be grateful that Michael took you back. You should be showing your gratitude every day, cooking him big meals and keeping this house cleaner—instead of pretending to be a great writer."

"I don't pretend! I *am* a writer, and some people think pretty good."

Her grandma snorted loudly. "I know you, Marilyn, remember? I'm your mother. I remember how poor your schoolwork was. A tenth-grade dropout, and you call yourself a good writer."

Randi clapped a hand over her mouth. She had never known her mom had dropped out of school!

"But I did finish later! I took those correspondence courses and got my high school diploma. You know that."

"That's beside the point. This first book was a fluke, an accident. It'll never happen again. Get your head out of the clouds."

"You don't know what you're talking about." Randi had to strain to catch her mom's faint words. She sounded ready to cry.

"Well, Miss Marilyn, you'd better be careful, that's all I can say. Or your handsome husband will up and leave *you* one of these fine days!"

Suddenly aware of how long she had eavesdropped, Randi slipped out of the house, careful to latch the back door without making a sound. In order to give them time to cool off, she played hide'n'seek with Meggie in the backyard for ten minutes before telling her Grandma was there.

When she and Meggie did step into the kitchen, it was quiet. Randi detected an uneasy truce. Stiff-backed, her mom ripped and tore salad greens at the sink, not even turning around when they let the door slam.

"Come on, Meggie. Grandma's in the living room." Randi smoothed Meggie's flyaway curls, then led her down the hall.

"Hi, Grandma!" Meggie hurled herself into her grandmother's outstretched arms. "When did you get here? Didn't Grandpa come this time, either? I was playing with T.C. Want to go see him?"

"In a minute." Grandma Dickson pulled Meggie down onto her lap. "My, you're growing. All ready for school to start?"

"Yup. I know my address and phone number, and Randi got me a cat bookbag!" Fidgeting, she brushed at her shirt front, which was covered with T.C.'s hair.

"That reminds me." Grandma dug deep into her shopping bag. "I know it won't be cold yet for months, but I made you these to keep away the frostbite this winter." She pulled out a hand-knitted purple scarf set. Soon Meggie was wrapped up till only her eyes peeked out between the hat and scarf.

"Ooh, pretty!" Meggie danced and twirled around the room, the tassels on the scarf slapping Randi's nose as she flew by. "I'm going to show Mommy."

After Meggie disappeared down the hall, Grandma Dickson resumed her knitting. "Now that we're alone, I want to know how things are going."

"What do you mean?" Randi asked, edging toward the doorway.

Grandma peered at her sharply. "You know what I mean—with your mother back."

"Okay, I guess." Randi measured her words carefully. "Meggie's not so upset anymore. She and Mom do things together. And Dad doesn't make fun of Mom's writing like he used to." When her grandma's eyebrows shot up, Randi hurried to add, "I don't mean he *really* made fun of her. He just teased her a little, but she didn't like it."

Grandma Dickson snorted. "I'll never understand Marilyn wanting to be a *writer*! Where'd she get such a highfalutin' idea? It's pure nonsense." The knitting needles flashed in and out.

"Why is it nonsense? Her book got published. She had an autograph party and everything." Randi gripped the back of a chair in surprise. Had *she* said that? Had she actually defended her mother's right to do what she wanted? She couldn't believe it!

"Have you read the book?" Grandma asked suspiciously.

"Well, no, but my friends bought it. I can show you a copy."

"No need. I don't intend to encourage Marilyn's foolishness. Someone has to talk some sense into her." She pointed a sharp knitting needle at Randi. "No good ever comes from trying to rise above your natural station in life. You remember that." She hunched over, knitting and purling furiously.

Randi shifted from one foot to another, grateful when Meggie bounced back into the room to announce lunch.

All during her mom's quiche and salad, Grandma Dickson's words went round and round in Randi's mind. The more she thought, the more amazed she was that her mom had even tried to write a book. Grandma had obviously been against it. Her dad had just laughed at the idea. In spite of them both, her mom had still tried to "rise above her natural station in life," as Grandma put it.

Randi studied her mother's pale face. It must have been hard to shake off her past, then shape her life into something she really wanted. Grudgingly, Randi had to admire her for that.

Some two hours later, agonizing hours to Randi, the taxi pulled away from the curb, taking Grandma Dickson back to the bus depot. With lips pressed together, Randi's mom disappeared into her office and shut the door. Looking bewildered, Meggie wrapped the tattered yellow scarf around her hand like a thick bandage and sat outside the closed door.

"Shall we go get T.C.?" Randi asked, trying to make Meggie smile. "It's probably cooler in the basement than in the garage."

Meggie nodded. "Can we play with him in the backyard first?" she asked. Going through the kitchen, she grabbed two cookies from the plate still on the table, then stuffed a third one in her mouth.

"Sure, we can stay outside awhile."

While watching Meggie and T.C. roll around on the grass, Randi leaned back on her elbows. The sun's heat soaking through her shirt loosened the painful knots in her stomach. Her mind drifting, she listened to the far-off hum of bees.

"Hey, look what I caught!" Meggie's voice pierced the still afternoon air.

"What is it?" Randi blinked and shaded her eyes.

Meggie stumbled across the yard to her and dropped down on her knees. "An orange butterfly with tiny black-and-white spots on it." She opened her cupped hands just a crack to let Randi peer inside. Wings folded, the trapped butterfly lay still.

Then, in one smooth motion, Meggie lifted her plump arms high in the air. For Randi, the moment was captured as permanently as if on film. She watched as Meggie slowly opened her hands and let the butterfly go free. They gazed upward together until it was a mere pinpoint of orange light against the sky.

Then the butterfly was gone.

Randi leaned back, still holding her breath. With a flash of insight, she finally knew what she had to do.

During Grandma's visit that day, things had started to make sense. She'd seen her mother in a new light; there was a different side to Marilyn Dickson McBride besides the self-assured writer who autographed books and had her own office. She was still a *child* to her own mother, a mother who wanted to tie her to a past she had tried to overcome.

Randi pulled up a blade of grass and slowly shredded it. When she was grown up, would it be like that? Would she still be fighting with her mother like her mom did with Grandma Dickson? She hoped not. Who wanted a whole lifetime of that?

Her mom had gone from a high school dropout to a published writer. Her past failures hadn't determined her life. In the same way, Randi saw that the painful past year didn't have to shape *her* future, either—or her feelings about her mother—for the rest of her life.

No matter what she had done, Marilyn McBride would always be her mother, the only mom she would ever have. Somehow, she had to separate her mom from the deep hurt she had caused—and simply let the hurt go.

Randi rolled over on her stomach, resting her chin on her folded hands. She was so tired of always being angry. It was *exhausting*. Letting go of the pain and resentment wouldn't be easy, though—she wasn't kidding herself. But if she didn't do it, Randi knew she was trapped, and her hate would become her future. She knew now that she didn't want that.

The only way to reverse directions was to release her mother from her past mistakes, just as Meggie had freed the butterfly.

But can I do it? Randi asked herself. *Is it really possible?*

The scars from the past year were deep. Randi would always believe that her mother had had no right to run away. Surely she could have "found herself" without tearing the family apart.

"Come on, Randi!" Meggie yelled, scooping T.C. up in her arms. "Let's go have some more lemonade."

"Okay." Randi stood and stretched, feeling fifty pounds lighter. What a relief to come to a decision at last, for better or worse. Whether her mom deserved it or not—

and regardless if she asked for it—Randi would try to forgive her.

For everyone's sake, including her own, it was time to put the past in the past.

11

∎

INNOCENT BYSTANDERS

Two weeks later Randi got another letter from Alex. Her mouth fell open when she read it.

> *Did you drop dead or what, McBride? This is the third letter I've written since you answered, and the last.*
>
> *I know things are the pits for you at home, but life isn't exactly paradise here, either. Dad hasn't found a job yet. He yells at Lois every night, then slams out of the house. I can't wait to get out of here.*
>
> *But why am I telling you all this? You don't care.*

With hands that shook, Randi slipped the unsigned letter back into the envelope. How could she have been so unfeeling? She had *meant* to answer Alex's last two letters, but so many things had interfered. Besides, for most of the summer she had felt lousy.

101

Still, Randi knew there was no good excuse for hurting Alex's feelings. He had always been there for her, especially during the months after her mom had run away. Sick or not, she should have made time to write. Alex really was her best friend, and she had let him down.

"Miranda! Are you ready to go?" her mom called from the kitchen.

"Just a minute!"

That morning Randi and her mom were going shopping for new school clothes, but as soon as she got home she would sit down and answer Alex. Maybe a nice, long, newsy letter would show him she hadn't meant to ignore him. She would look for a funny card at the mall for him, too.

Randi yanked a brush through her hair, mad at herself for what she had done. It had been a hard summer, but she hadn't meant to hurt Alex at all. He had just been an innocent bystander.

A sudden thought struck her, and she stopped in mid-stroke. "Did *that* happen to Mom, too?" she whispered, staring into the mirror.

Had her mom had so many problems—enough to make her run away—that she had accidentally hurt Meggie and Randi in the bargain? She dropped her brush with a clatter. Maybe her mother hadn't meant to hurt *them*, either, just like Randi hadn't meant to hurt Alex.

"Hurry up, Randi!" Meggie yelled.

"Coming!" Randi retrieved her brush, smoothed down the rest of her spiky hair, then hurried to the kitchen where her mom and Meggie were waiting.

Randi eyed her little sister. "Did you go to the bathroom yet?"

"I don't have to." Meggie pranced toward the door, the yellow scarf hanging from her shorts like a tail. "Let's go."

"Not till you go to the bathroom. March." Randi pointed down the hall. "Remember the last time on the bus? I didn't think you were going to make it."

Meggie grinned suddenly. "Oh, yeah. I forgot." She dashed down the hall, her tail flying.

"You're going to be a good mother," her mom said. "You've got all the right instincts."

Not like some people I could mention, Randi thought with a flash. Shaking her head, she reminded herself that she wasn't going to think like that anymore. Instead she forced a smile. "Meggie's a good kid."

Soon they were speeding across town in her mom's little car. In the mall the smell of caramel corn was strong, and Meggie pulled them toward the store. "Let's get some caramel corn. I'm starving."

Marilyn shook her head, then laughed suddenly. "Sure. Why not?" She stepped up to the counter and ordered three small boxes, then handed each girl a box.

Meggie dug in, crunching noisily, but Randi was surprised at the angry words that nearly choked her. Her mom hadn't even asked if she wanted any or not. Randi carried the unopened box as they strolled down the mall, window shopping.

"Aren't you hungry?" her mom asked.

Before Randi could answer, Meggie spoke up. Three popcorn kernels blew out of her full mouth. "She doesn't like it. Randi always gets cheese corn."

"Really? Don't you like caramel corn?"

Randi shrugged. "It's okay. I'm not hungry." *You've been gone so long you don't remember anything about me,* she muttered inwardly. Passing a trash bin, she tossed the full box through the open lid.

They continued down the mall, admiring the fall clothes in store windows and surprised at the Halloween costumes already on display. Meggie chattered nonstop between them, but Randi barely heard a word. It took all her effort to keep smiling. She still intended to let go of her resentment, but it was going to take a lot of practice.

"Ooohh, look! I want to try that on! Just for fun." Randi glanced up as her mom stopped in front of a fur coat store. "Who knows? Maybe I'll buy one soon." She pointed at the CHRISTMAS LAYAWAY sign in the window.

Inside, her mom giggled like a little girl as she tried on one coat after another, the fur ranging from glossy black to snowy white. Some coats were nearly floor-length, while others were no more than fuzzy jackets. Her mom paraded back and forth in front of the glittering oval mirrors, while Meggie clapped and chomped on her caramel corn. Embarrassed, Randi saw an aggravated saleslady point them out to a well-dressed man, probably the manager.

Randi studied her mom as she minced back and forth in a leopard coat. You'd think she didn't have a care in the world. Not like *some* people, who had to worry about ulcers.

Randi shook her head slowly. *What's the matter with me?* she asked herself. She had decided to forgive her mom, and she honestly meant it. *So why do I still feel so mad?* Evidently, the hate habit was hard to break.

It reminded her of last year when she had decided to stop biting her fingernails. She had had to break that habit over and over again before she finally quit altogether. She guessed forgiving her mom was going to be the same—a long process. Maybe the key to burying the past was to pretend it had never happened. She would turn the clock back a year and mentally erase all the pain in between. At least, it was worth a try.

"Guess we'd better go," her mom said, hanging up the last fur jacket. "That was fun! I feel just like a kid again."

With new resolve, Randi got slowly to her feet. Recalling

shopping trips from other years, she tried to recapture some of the fun.

Meggie yanked on her mom's arm. "Remember you always gave me pennies to throw in the fountain?"

"The one by Sebastian's?" Her mother's eyes lit up. "Do they still have all the colored lights under the water?"

"Remember when I fell in last year?" Meggie asked. "That was funny."

"You didn't *fall* in," Randi said, ruffling up her curls. "When I wasn't looking, you climbed in to fish out the money in the bottom."

"I want to throw some pennies in again!"

They left the store, Meggie holding fast to her mother's and sister's hands. If Randi really concentrated, she could almost pretend they were a normal family.

Passing a card shop, Randi slowed down. "I want to get a card."

"Who for?" Meggie asked.

"Alex." Randi caught her mother's surprised glance. "His letter sounded depressed. I thought I'd get a funny card to cheer him up."

"That's thoughtful. What's the matter with Alexander? Or do you mind my asking?"

His runaway parent has gone bananas, too, Randi almost blurted out. She turned abruptly, before her mom read the thought in her face. "He just misses his friends, I think."

She couldn't tell her mom the real problem. She knew Alex considered it private. Anyway, talking about parents who had walked out was hardly the way to put the past behind her.

A few minutes later she found the perfect card. A sad-eyed moose with drooping antlers was on the front. Inside it read: *I've moosed you. Hurry back.* Tucking the card in her purse, she trailed her mom down the mall. Meggie had run ahead to the fountain, waving two pennies high over her head.

"Wait! Be sure to make a wish first," their mom called.

"I did. I wished for T.C. to have some baby kittens." Meggie pulled back her arm and let the pennies fly.

Her mom chuckled. "I'm afraid that's one wish that will never come true," she whispered to Randi. "Isn't T.C. a tomcat?"

"Yes, but there's no point in telling Meggie. She has a lot of faith in this fountain, especially after . . ." She broke off, biting her lip.

"Especially after what?"

"After we came here last spring. She brought all the money from her piggy bank and threw it in." Randi stared into the foaming water, colored by the rotating red and blue lights.

"Why did you let her do that?"

"I couldn't stop her!" Randi erupted angrily. Two shoppers nearby turned and stared at her. Breathing deeply, she forced her voice lower. "Meggie threw in her money, then wished that you'd come home. A month later you did, so she thinks this fountain is magic." Randi turned and started toward the mall exit.

"Where're you going?" her mom demanded. "We haven't bought your school clothes yet."

Ignoring her, Randi broke into a run. She swiped at the tears that threatened to spill over. The fountain had brought it all back again, in living color. She would never forget seeing Meggie throw in all her money, so confident that it would bring their mother home. Then came the long nights of holding her, while Meggie cried because her mom hadn't appeared right away.

It was no use, Randi thought. She couldn't possibly

pretend that nothing had ever happened. Something terrible *had* happened, and she would always have the scars.

Outside, Randi turned away from the parking lot. She glimpsed the city bus pulling around the corner and sprinted toward the bus stop. Panting, she arrived in time to follow the last person in line up the steps.

Inside, she sank wearily onto a hot plastic seat. Glancing out the window, she spotted Meggie and her mom halfway across the parking lot. Randi turned her back to the window as the bus pulled into traffic. Why had she bothered to come? Evidently there was more to "forgiving and forgetting" than just pretending nothing had happened. The hurt wasn't going to vanish so quickly—or so easily.

Randi slumped farther down into the seat. *What am I going to do now?* she wondered, picking at a dried wad of bubble gum on the seat ahead of her. "There has to be some way out of this mess."

Glancing at the funny card in her sack, her thoughts turned to Alex. If he hadn't told her that she'd hurt his feelings, Randi might never have guessed. Alex could have kept quiet and let his anger grow instead, finally ruining their friendship. Randi was glad he hadn't. This way she would be able to apologize when she sent him the card. Alex wouldn't hold a grudge, she knew; they would be friends just as if nothing had happened.

Randi shifted uncomfortably in her sticky seat, embarrassed now at the way she had run away from the mall. She had acted like a baby. This forgiveness thing wasn't working at all, at least not in the way she planned.

Maybe she'd have to show some guts like Alex and be honest with her mom, before healing could begin. Unless she confronted her mom about the hurt she had caused—whether accidentally or not—things probably would never be right again.

Back home in the empty house, Randi went straight to her room to write a note in Alex's card.

Dear Alex,

I don't blame you for being mad. I counted on your letters to cheer me up this summer, but I let you down. I'm really sorry. I guess I was wrapped up in my problems with Mom.

How's your dad? Did he find a job yet? It must be hard when somebody younger takes your job away. Even so, I bet he never meant to hurt you this summer. I think he's too worried right now to think about anybody else. Maybe he's doing the best he can.

Maybe last year my mom did the best she could, too. I don't know. When Grandma Dickson came a while back, I learned some things that might explain why Mom left. I'll tell you about it when you get back.

Remember when you said I should put the past behind me? I'm trying, but it's pretty hard. And slow. I guess once you've been sliced and diced inside, it takes a long time to heal.

I won't know if it'll work until I talk with Mom, but I'm not sure I can. I wouldn't know where to start. She honestly doesn't think she did anything wrong, so would talking even do any good?

I guess it depends on how much I want her back in my life again. I've trained myself to get along okay without her.

Thanks for writing even when I didn't. I hope your dad is okay soon. I can't wait till you get home next week.

Apologetically,

Randi

12

■

THE FIRST STEP

The next night Randi lay in bed, her heart pounding as she listened to Meggie's soft snoring. The house was so still, silent except for the hum of the rotating fan on her desk. Her dad was working late at the store's Midnight Madness sale, and her mom was waiting up for him.

Flopping over, Randi peered at her clock's lighted dial: 11:13. She had been rolling around in bed since ten and still couldn't relax. If only she could turn off her mind!

In broad daylight, her intentions concerning her mother were so good. She was *determined* to put the past behind her. Dealing with her feelings at night, though, was a totally different story. When the sun went down, the old hurts rushed back, like ghosts that only haunt after dark.

Randi clutched Muddy to her knotted stomach. No matter how good her intentions, she couldn't magically erase the past. But maybe she could take some steps to deal with it.

With a sigh, she swung her legs over the edge of the

bed. Unless she was willing to be honest with her mother—the way Alex had been with her—neither of them would be free of the past or have a chance to be close again in the future.

She padded down the darkened hall, aware of pages rustling in the living room. Peeking around the corner, she saw her mother curled up on the couch, reading a magazine. Randi cleared her throat.

Her mom jumped. "Oh, Miranda! You scared me." Raising one eyebrow, she asked, "Are you feeling all right?"

"Yeah, I'm fine." Randi hung back in the doorway, surprised to see she was still clutching her stuffed monkey. "I just wanted to . . . I thought maybe we could . . ." Her voice trailed off. Now that she was ready to clear the air, the words stuck in her throat. She dropped Muddy to the floor, where he landed in a heap.

"Maybe we could what?" her mom asked hopefully, closing her magazine.

"Um, well, I'm kind of hungry. Could I make some pudding?" Randi blurted out the first thing that popped into her mind.

"That sounds good. Your dad won't be home for another hour yet, and I'd love the company." Her mom paused. "That is, if you want some help in the kitchen."

"Okay." Avoiding her mother's gaze, Randi went to the kitchen and got ingredients out for pudding. She measured two cups of milk into a glass dish to heat in the microwave.

Her mom measured cocoa, corn starch, and sugar into another bowl. When the microwave beeped, Randi added the dry ingredients and whipped out the lumps. After another three minutes' cooking, it was thick and bubbly.

Randi carried their bowls of pudding to the table, then poured two glasses of milk. "All done," she said, suddenly embarrassed.

"Wait a second." Her mom reached into the cupboard for a handful of miniature marshmallows. "When I was little, I used to love marshmallows in warm pudding. I'd bury them at the bottom and eat them when they started to melt." She tossed a few into her bowl, and the rest into Randi's.

Randi pushed each marshmallow under the surface of her hot pudding. She stirred back and forth, drawing designs on the top with her spoon.

"I thought you were hungry," her mom said a few minutes later. "Or was the pudding just an excuse?"

"An excuse?"

"I had the feeling you wanted to talk about something."

It's now or never, Randi decided, taking a deep breath. "There *was* something I wanted to say." She groped for the right words. "But, well, it's just that. . . ."

The silence drew out. The only sounds in the kitchen were the humming of the refrigerator and the clunk of the ice maker. Waiting, her mother quietly ate one chocolate-covered marshmallow after another.

Finally Randi took the plunge. It felt like diving headfirst into a deep hole. "When you came home this summer, I was ready to hate you for the rest of my life." She looked her mother in the eye. "But I don't want to anymore. I thought maybe we should talk."

Her mom dropped her spoon with a clatter. She let her breath out slowly. "You're right. It's a talk we've put off too long." She started to reach across the table to Randi, hesitated, then pulled her hand back.

Randi stirred her pudding slowly, blending the melted marshmallow streaks into the chocolate. "I don't think you know how bad you hurt us by leaving."

"But I *do* know," her mom protested. "It's just that I knew you'd be able to take care of yourselves and each other. I was right, wasn't I?"

"What choice did we have when you ripped apart our family?" Randi snapped. "Just because we survived doesn't mean it didn't hurt! I felt like dying!"

Her mom looked genuinely surprised. "But you always said you were doing fine. Even after I came home, it was obvious you didn't need me at all."

Randi remembered the early weeks of struggling to pretend nothing was bothering her. "I didn't want to give you the satisfaction of knowing I hurt that much. Or *cared* that much. But I did."

"Then why. . . ."

"Why pretend everything was fine?" Randi's voice was barely more than a whisper. "Somehow, if I handled all the cooking and cleaning, and gave you lots of time to write, it would prove it wasn't *my* fault if you left us again."

"Your fault? But you had nothing to do with my leaving last year. I thought you knew that." Her mom shoved back her chair and gripped the edge of the table. "It had nothing to do with you," she repeated quietly. "It was *my* problem, and I had to work it out."

"Maybe, but you sure made it *my* problem," Randi said, slapping the table with the palm of her hand. The bowls jumped. "You left *me* to run the house, to be Meggie's mother, to figure everything out by myself! I hated what you did to me and Meggie. You could have stayed here and worked out your problems."

"Every time I talked to your father last year, he said you were coping marvelously. 'Randi stepped right in and filled your shoes.' Those were his words." Marilyn knelt down beside Randi's chair. "I knew my leaving would be a shock at first, but I didn't think it would hurt that much." She reached out slowly and put a hand on Randi's shoulder.

Jerking aside, Randi brushed her hand off. "You didn't think it would hurt that much? Maybe you just didn't think at all."

Sighing, her mom took the empty milk glasses to the sink. She stared out the window into the dark backyard. "I wish I could turn the calendar back and change things, but I can't. I'm so sorry for what I put you through. I can see it hurt much more than I believed."

For a long moment, Randi sat ramrod stiff, wanting desperately to march out of the kitchen without another word. Giving up the last of her hate was harder than anything she'd ever done. Finally, she turned and looked at her mom, who stood hunched over the sink. The last thing she felt like doing was forgiving her. Evidently it was a matter of actions first—not feelings.

Like a wooden soldier, Randi walked across the kitchen and put her hand on top of her mother's. It wasn't much, but it was a start.

Her mom glanced up quickly, then gripped Randi's hand in hers. "I don't know if you can believe me, Miranda, but I promise never to do anything like that again."

Randi looked into her mother's eyes, surprised at the pain she saw there. Maybe her mom had been hurt by the past year, too. Things could never go back to where they had been before she ran away. They would just have to work with what they had now and make a new beginning.

"I believe you, Mom." Randi felt like someone who had just survived surgery to remove what was killing her. Now she had to wait for the healing to begin. "I do believe you. We can start over."

Her mom squeezed Randi's hand. "Let's take our pudding into the living room where it's cozier. I *do* want to start over. There are so many things I wanted to ask you— like what your best subject was last year, and why Alex is a special friend, and all kinds of things."

Randi followed her mom into the living room. "There are things I want to ask you, too. Like what it's like to autograph a book for somebody. And why you wanted to write a book in the first place. And, well, I'd like to read it, too."

Her mom spooned up a huge mouthful of pudding. "I just happen to have an extra copy. It's on top of the filing cabinet in my office."

"Okay. I'll get it later." Randi stooped to pick Muddy up from where she had dropped him, then sat Indian-style on the floor.

Her mom smiled. "I was surprised to see you still had that old monkey. He's traveled a lot of miles."

"He does look a little beat up," Randi agreed. "I found him in a box last winter up in the closet. What a dumb name I gave him. Muddy—I guess because he was the color of mud."

"No, don't you remember?" Her mom reached down and took the lumpy animal. "I made him for you out of your dad's socks when you were about three. You'd been really sick with the flu, and I wanted to cheer you up. It took most of one day to sew Muddy. Whenever you got sick after that you and Muddy curled up together on the couch." She polished the cracked button eyes and nose.

"But why the name?" Randi asked.

"After I finished sewing him, you asked what day it was." Marilyn McBride patted the monkey's bottom and handed him back. "When I told you it was Monday, you said that would be his name. Only when you said it, the name came out Muddy."

Randi sat Muddy on the floor, balanced on his tail. So that was why she had saved Muddy all these years. No wonder she had reached for him this past year when the stomach cramps had twisted her into knots of pain. In her past, he had stood for love.

Just minutes later, Randi was surprised to hear her dad's key in the kitchen door. The clock on the mantle read

12:20. "Oops. Guess I'd better get to bed." She hoped the sale had been a big hit, but she didn't want to hear all about it just then. " 'Night, Mom."

She carried the empty bowls to the kitchen, then quickly kissed her dad good night. Going past her mom's office, she stepped in and took the copy of *Love Under Glass*.

Crawling into bed, she snapped on the dim reading light above her headboard. Her sense of relief after talking with her mom had left her limp. Even though Randi knew an uphill climb was still ahead of her, she had made a start. She had taken that first step. Finally the worst was behind her.

Even her stomach felt better. The cramps had relaxed some, although the pain wasn't gone by a long shot. Dr. Benoit had said this kind of problem took a while to go away. Yet Randi felt hopeful that it would, in time.

With the tip of her finger, she traced the gold letters of the book's title. Besides her mom's new career, Randi had to admit a few other good things had come out of the last year's upheaval.

She listed them on her fingers. She could now cook a lot, and some of the dishes tasted pretty good. She could clean the house from top to bottom in one day. And she wasn't scared anymore to call doctors or baby-sitters. Most importantly, she had grown close to Meggie during the past year. Maybe, if she concentrated on these good things, the bad memories would fade faster.

Shivering, Randi pulled Grandma's patchwork quilt up to her chin. Fingering the old material, she studied its crazy design. Like a quilt-maker, Randi was determined to take the scraps of her summer—the pretty and the ugly— and make them into something useful. Maybe even beautiful.

Scrunching down on her pillow, Randi opened the cover of the brand-new book and began to read.

115

H 733

①

'89

DATE DUE

JUL 3 0 1981			
AG 29 '91			
DE 0 4 '81			
JUN 2 0 '95			

DEMCO 38-297